Reign

By Tristan Day

PublishAmerica
Baltimore

First printing

ISBN: 1-60672-100-3
PUBLISHED BY PUBLISHAMERICA, LLLP
www.publishamerica.com
Baltimore

Printed in the United States of America

Hi mom!

STEP 1
MORGAN

"With the passing of six long days, the Master forged the World, and breathed life into the first of its people. He called him Angel. And into him, He poured a power like the universe had never known. A piece of the Master's own essence rested within the Angel. A piece of His kindness. His benevolence. His generosity. And His wrath…"

"Continue with the next line, Mr. Craft."

Young Morgan Craft could barely hear the old, rickety voice of the man that had just called out his name. He was far too busy surfing through his own dreams to care for whatever the grey-bearded Mr. English was babbling on about on that early morning. His head tucked under his book, lying on one side against the wooden table, he sat there, half-asleep, not wanting to answer.

"Mr. Craft," the teacher persisted.

Morgan finally lifted his head from its comfortable spot on the table and, through a veil of his own messy, blue hair, he could see the other students. They all sat around that long table, looking back and forth between him and Mr. English, wondering what was going to happen next.

Morgan could not help but smile at the sight of it. The nervous faces of all those clean, pampered children of noble families, brought here to learn alongside Prince Morgan. Each one unsure of what might happen to this sapphire-eyed young man, now that he had been discovered as having not been listening.

"What?"

It was the only thing Morgan could think to say. It seemed the most sensible thing, at the time. After all, he still had no idea what that old crow of a man wanted, let alone what it had to do with him. Unfortunately, it seemed that it was most definitely the wrong thing to say to Mr. English on this morning. The last day of the first week.

"Continue reading, with the next line," Mr. English said, one last time.

"I'm sorry, Mr. English," Morgan answered sarcastically. "I seem to be missing the page in my book. Maybe you could read it for me. I could never match your eloquence with the Angelic Text."

Mr. English closed his eyes behind those old, rusted glasses of his and sighed. But when he opened them again, a chill fell over the room. Several children around the table could not help but flinch at the sight of them. Those immense things that suddenly exploded out from behind him like fireworks. A pair of Angelic Wings stretched out from his back, nearly touching either side of the classroom. And, from those wings, an emanation of power swept through the place. The windows snapped themselves shut. The lights in the walls began to flicker.

The students looked upon Mr. English nervously. They had not reached the age of 17, and thus none of them had Angelic Wings yet. But they could feel the power flowing from the cranky old man, and knew not to cross his gaze.

Mr. English tossed his book at the table and it shot clear across the room, stopping in the middle of the air, just in front of young Morgan's face. The cover split open and the pages flipped until they reached the correct passage. In a single wave, the faces of the students all turned back toward Morgan.

Silence fell upon the room, as the students watched and waited to see what would happen next, to the boy at the end of the table. But Morgan snatched the book out of the air with little hesitation, and with a loud clap, the book was closed again. Eyes all across the room widened with muted surprise.

"I have a better idea," Morgan said, before hopping right up onto the edge of the table. "I think we should learn something else today. Like…" He paused for a moment to think. "Balance."

Mr. English clutched a fist behind his back. "Balance?" he asked, in irritation.

"Yes, balance. It's as important as anything else."

Morgan took the brick-red book of Angelic Text and placed it on top of his head. He then proceeded to walk slowly across the table. A few smiles began to creep up on the faces of the other students as they watched him stumble here and there, making sure not to step on anything important, trying to balance the book on his head without touching it.

Mr. English looked as though his head might pop under the strain. His wings reverted to a pocket of nothingness behind him as he stood there, unable to do anything. Morgan Craft was not just another noble-born student in his classroom. He was a prince. Adopted son of the King of Moralvia. A single word from the young fool could mean the end of his career in the royal service. And so he stood there, grinding his teeth, as a wingless 15-year-old trampled over the table with the Angelic Text on his head.

By now, Morgan had even gotten a few giggles out of the room—all those uptight sons and daughters of nobles, laughing. Perhaps school didn't have to be as boring as he had always thought it was. But then, as the door to the room swung open, and he saw who it was that had entered the room, he thought again.

"Come along, Morgan," King Brennan spoke. Faces dropped all around him as everyone began to bow. Morgan turned to face his brown-bearded father with a smile, as innocent-looking as he could force across his face. Fortunately for him, the king was not in the mood for yelling.

~ * ~

The green light panels in the walls glowed brightly as Morgan walked through the halls of the castle with his father. King Brennan stood tall, with an imposing swagger. To many, he was the most powerful Angel in the land. Those who fell into his favor were blessed with lavish kindness. Those who fell out of favor suffered in ways best left unspoken of. But to Morgan, he was simply his father.

"You might think about setting a better example," Brennan said at last.

"For whom?" Morgan asked, though he probably knew the answer already.

"For the other students. Mr. English is trying to teach you something. And your disruptions don't help matters."

"If the old cow didn't pick on me all the time. I think he's angry at me for being a prince—"

"Mr. English isn't picking on you. If anything, he gives you more attention because he knows you need it. Everyone must learn the Angelic Text and understand its meaning. Without that, you could become as bad as those miscreant heathens in the streets, who don't know which way is up."

"Can I visit the city tomorrow?"

Brennan sighed. The boy was only two years away from developing his wings, and still he had trouble keeping to the subject at hand.

Before Brennan could utter a response, a warrior in red approached from around the corner with a bow. It was Randir, high-ranking Royal Guardian of Moralvia.

"King Brennan," Randir began. "It seems we've had another…incident with a few peasants outside the castle gates. Another protest."

"I care not to hear the ramblings of fools that follow false principles. Execute Order 13."

"…Order 13, sir?"

"I will not allow those faithless idiots to infect the harmony of our loyal citizens with their backward lifestyle. With their thieving, and their war, and their Alorium. They must be made an example of. Now, Randir, Execute Order 13. Now!"

"Yes, my king." In a moment, Randir was gone.

Morgan was confused. He paid as little attention as possible to his father's royal dealings (much to the king's disappointment), but one word he spoke stood out in his mind. "Alorium." Morgan knew he had heard the term once before, in an old poem about a great war, but still was unsure of its meaning. He would not have time to ask it, because his father was quickly being called away by other servants.

Before rushing off to tend to his duties, King Brennan turned to his son and rested his huge hands upon the young man's shoulders with a smile.

"Do not think that these distractions will make me forget what we were speaking about. Sometime in the future, all that I have will belong to you. And if you do not learn what is there for you to learn, the kingdom will fall into ruin. You don't want that, do you?"

"No," Morgan said, almost mechanically.

"I love you."

Brennan smiled at his son and walked off. It was rare that the king actually spoke those words to him, though he showed his feelings through his kindness.

"And don't forget your studies," the king's voice rang out from down the hall.

Morgan frowned. The last thing he wanted to do for the rest of the day was study those boring Texts. But when day passed into night...that was another story all together....

~ * ~

Morgan placed an ear up to the door and listened. Silence. Good. They were all asleep.

Morgan made his way quietly over to his bedroom window, the light of the moons hanging in the night sky pouring in through the glass. He carefully opened the windows and breathed in the cool breeze. He looked down to see the city below.

The castle stood atop the great Rising Mountain, which had been lifted by Angelic air hundreds of years ago. The entire mountain now towered high in the air, floating among the clouds, over the silvery city that rested below. At night, when the moons were full, and the people of the kingdom slept, this place was his secret playground. For no one knew that one thing about him which he kept from all the others, even the few classmates that he might sometimes call friends. No one but him...

Morgan crept up the wall, placing his feet onto the edge of the open window ledge. He could feel the breeze rustling through the black clothes he had dressed in. He looked straight down, where all he could see was clouds.

And then Morgan jumped.

A cool night breeze changed to a fierce wind, which whipped through Morgan's hair as he dropped down alongside the wall of the castle. His weight ripped him out of the air with frightening force. He descended further and further down through a layer of clouds and emerged below them to see a huge formation of sharp rocks. Morgan's eyes widened with a rush of fear as he realized he was about to slam down into the rocks along the edge of Rising Mountain.

But just moments before Morgan hit the rocks, a wondrous pair of wings burst out of his back and carried him swooping over the mountain on a sudden rush of wind. Morgan let out a great laugh, as the wind flapped through the blue feathers of his wings, gliding him across the night sky. His secret wings, which no one else his age possessed.

Down from the Rising Mountain and over the houses and between buildings, Morgan flew. He spun through the air, with a freedom like he could never know during the day. During the time of school, and learning, and text, and royalty, and boredom. But out here, in the sky, he was free from it all.

Morgan made his way beyond the central city, across the lake. He smiled down at his own reflection as he flew over it, and ran his finger along the water until at last he came to the old teahouse. It was one of the few places he still had not seen. And it was time to change that.

~ * ~

Simon Donnigan struck a match across an old tree and watched the flame ignite at its tip, glowing majestically amid the darkness as he used it to light the paperleaf in his mouth. Simon breathed in deeply and let out a cloud of smoke that fogged up his glasses. His long blonde hair flowed gently in the breeze as he walked slowly, smoking his paperleaf with the four others in his unit. It had been a long night, and they were ready to return to their homes.

But then Simon stopped as he felt something in the air. He turned just in time to see through the haze of smoke the tiny image of an Angel in black flying over the nearby lake, toward the teahouse. Something about this made his wings shiver with suspicion.

~ * ~

Morgan ruffled quietly through the storage room of the old teahouse looking for sweets. He could not believe it. He knew that the place was called a "teahouse" but how could the entire place hold nothing but tea? Tea bags. Tea leaves. Tea cups. But no candies, or cookies, or anything.

Morgan stopped for a moment when he thought he heard the owners of the house moving around upstairs, but then decided that it was just his imagination, from fear of being caught. They must have been fast asleep by now. No one should be awake this late, especially after the king's curfew.

Finally, Morgan landed on the only thing he could find of interest. A special tea his father drank sometimes. One that he was always forbidden to drink, because it makes you insanely drunk. What luck. His father was not going to be around when he drank it. He grabbed a few bags of it, stuffed them inside a pocket and headed out the door.

Morgan closed the front door to the teahouse and smiled as he hopped up into the air, conjuring his wings for flight. But before he could fly away, he felt a set of fingers lock themselves around his ankle, holding him there in the air. Morgan turned over his shoulder to see a man in a long, black leather coat with hay-colored hair, refusing to let go of him.

"What are you doing out at night?" Simon spoke, with authority. "Curfew began many hours ago."

Morgan quickly realized that the man did not recognize him under the veil of night. And, if he wanted to keep his secrets—about his royal status, and about his wings—he would have to get out of there. Quickly.

Simon felt a strange flicker of power that surged through the boy's ankle, forcing itself free of his grip. Simon gasped in surprise as the boy went sailing away from the teahouse at incredible speeds, carving a wave of water across the surface of the lake as he flew. But Simon was not going to release him so easily. His golden wings reached forth from his back, darting him across the lake toward the boy.

Morgan stopped just a moment later, when he realized that one of Simon's men was standing there on the surface of the water, waiting for him. And another to his left. And another to his right. Morgan looked up into the air, and the last Angel stood hanging in the sky above, the light of the moon glowing through his feathers. Nowhere to run.

Simon pulled a small ivory tablet from his coat and raised it before him. The carvings in the tablet were unmistakable. It was the seal of the local law enforcers. Morgan had not realized that they patrolled this late at night.

"By order of the king, I place you under arrest, for thieving," Simon announced. With a nod of his head, he signaled the other four officers to take the boy.

Morgan looked around in uncertainty as one officer descended from above, while three others approached from every side, with Simon waiting patiently behind. They began to close in…

"*No!*" Morgan shouted. The sound of his voice seemed to burst out of him like a strong wind through an open window.

Simon watched in astonishment as an incredible force exploded from the boy's outstretched wings, and all four of his men were sent flying back in different directions. Morgan let out a furious scream from some unimaginable place within him, as the officers went skidding across the surface of the lake, crashing into trees along the outskirts of the city, and falling out of sight.

Simon's eyes narrowed. Never had he seen an Angel that looked so young possess such power. But that was not his concern. He had a duty, and would not be kept from carrying it out.

Morgan instinctively leapt up toward Simon with ferocious strength, hurling his arms and fists at him. Simon's left hand whipped around him with unearthly speed, blocking the boy's undisciplined, unpracticed attacks one after another. But the strength that each attack packed was more than he was prepared for. Even he, with all his powers, knew that he had to be careful, even if he was facing a child, who had never fought a single battle.

Morgan's arms grew tired, as they ripped through the air hundreds of times in a matter of seconds, still hitting nothing but the backs of Simon's arms. At last, he darted backwards into the air. A bolt of blue lightning crackled between his fingers, and he released it, hoping that it would be enough to stop the officer. But Simon simply stood there, as he knew that the bolt would only hit the lake below him and dissipate, without hitting its target.

Simon looked up at Morgan and knew that he had no choice but to harm the boy. With great reluctance, he activated his Angelic gift. Focusing his spectral power into two fingers in his hand, he caused the lake below him to stir. An explosion of water rushed up around him and what remained was forged into a mighty liquid whip, the force of a hurricane bottled up inside every drop.

The stream of water lashed around him as he whirled his arm at his side, at last thrusting his hand up toward the blue-feathered boy. With that, the whip shot up into the air and struck its target.

Morgan let out a terrible scream as he felt a stream of water slash through the fabric of his shoulder with unimaginable pressure, sending him spiraling into the night air uncontrollably.

Never in his life had he experienced such an injury. Within that instant, he could feel the determination in the heart of the man. As if that water held more than just a painful sting, but a piece of his very essence.

A screen of water rushed up and covered the sky, blinding them both.

Morgan's vision strayed in and out, like his mind, as he struggled to make his way back to the castle, praying that the officer was too weak, or too stunned that his attack hadn't stopped him, to chase after him. The last thing Morgan could remember seeing before it all fell into shadow was the open window of his room…

~ * ~

Morgan was amazed.

As he stood there in front of the mirror, staring at his shoulder, he could hardly believe what he was seeing. The wound, which had felt so great that it might have very well ended his life just a few hours earlier, had now been reduced to a scar no larger than a pencil.

Morgan smiled. He knew that the power of an Angel's wings would allow you to heal faster than you would as a child, but had never suffered an injury so severe as to truly test it. But then again, no one his age had ever done what he had done.

"Morgan Craft!"

King Brennan's voice echoed halfway down the hall as he

barged right into his adopted son's bedroom. Morgan quickly conjured a shirt over himself to cover his injury, and tried to remember not to summon his wings now that he was back at home.

"Yes, father," he responded.

"You are an hour late for class. Mr. English is not going to be happy. And neither am I."

"I'm on my way now, father." Morgan had no idea he was that late. The healing must have taxed him more than he realized.

~ * ~

The day passed slowly as Morgan obsessed over the previous night's events. How exhilarated he felt. Others in his position might have been more frightened or nervous about what had happened, but all Morgan could think about was what wonderful mischief he was going to find himself in the next time he went out. He was so happy that he even read from the Angelic Text for the class, to the surprise of Mr. English.

But that night, when he placed his ear to the door and found that he heard nothing but the snoring of noblemen and servants tucked away in bed, he was done with texts. He was ready to begin another adventure.

Morgan hopped up into the window in his black clothes and looked out at the silver city below. With excitement in his eyes, he summoned his wings right then and there. But then…

"Morgan, are you awake?"

Morgan turned around anxiously and realized too late that his father had just barged into the room!

King Brennan looked upon him with stunned silence. The boy, whom he called his son, was in the window panel, with blue wings, ready to steal off into the night. This was not possible. No Angel receives wings until the age of 17. No Angel…

Morgan searched his father's eyes for answers. A sign that he knew, and understood. The look in his eyes that he had witnessed just a day earlier, when he told him those precious words, which he used so rarely. But he did not receive it. He got everything he needed to know with the one and only word that his father could bare to speak.

"Abomination…"

With tears in his eyes, Morgan turned and jumped out of the window, not knowing where he would fly.

But something stopped him. A powerful force that rippled out of the room, clutching onto him and refusing to let go. It was like a web of anger. As if anger was a tangible force that could wrap itself around him and hold him there. Morgan turned in the air and witnessed his father's wings snap out of his back. His wings were made of blackness, their feathers of bottomless, hate-filled shadow, piercing through every last inch of light in the room, until there was nothing but a void, slowing dragging Morgan in like an abyss…

~ * ~

As Morgan's thoughts drifted in and out of coherence, his eyes fluttered about behind his eyelids, his body struggling to recover from that terrible power that had crept over him. Amid the blurred darkness, he heard voices. Ones that belonged to his father. And his teacher. And royal guards.

"A child who is born with wings is against the intention of nature. A child who is born with wings is no Angel. He is abomination. Not among the Master's favored."

"Execute Order 13."

"But sir, are you certain?"

"I took pity on this child because his father abandoned his mother, and the mother died in childbirth. But I see now that it was a mistake. That… That creature is not my son."

"But sir… What if he is Aloriu—"

Morgan snapped back awake with the sound of Brennan's hand striking a soldier's face. The man fell to the ground just next to him, but quickly jumped back and bowed.

"I beg your forgiveness," the royal guard said. "I spoke inappropriately."

"Yes, you did," Mr. English said, pulling himself away from the pages of the Angelic Text in his hand. "I will speak to you at services tomorrow."

Morgan looked around and realized that he was inside a large chamber. A foul smell lingered in the air, the remnants of whatever awfulness had inhabited that room before he did. And next to him was a strange device, which he had never seen before. But he did remember reading about such things in old war poems. At the top of the machine, there was a sharp blade. And down below, there was a spot for a man to place his neck…

"That's what Order 13 is," Morgan spoke.

King Brennan turned toward the boy on his knees. With tears streaming down his face, Morgan slowly stood up and looked around at the seven or eight men in the room. Most of them were soldiers, doing their duty. A few of them looked saddened by his reaction. His father looked at him with trembling eyes.

"You intend to kill me," Morgan continued. "You wish to kill me because I am different from those other kids in my class. Me…. I'm fifteen years old…. Is your son really that offensive to your eyes, because he has wings?"

No servant dared speak. Not one among them could be sure what might be said next. King Brennan stood there for a moment, staring into the blue, tear-soaked eyes of the young man looking up at him. At last, he mustered four words…

"I…have no son."

King Brennan shut his eyes and rushed out the door, throwing a hand over his mouth in horror. It was equaled only by the horror of his abandoned son.

"No more lessons from the young prince?"

The voice came flapping from the gums of that old, grey-bearded teacher. Morgan turned toward him with a look no one had ever seen. Mr. English just smiled.

"No?" he asked, tauntingly. "How about a lesson on *balance*?

That sounds like something very important for a young boy to learn. Perhaps you could demonstrate for us."

Mr. English tossed the book down, and sent it floating over toward Morgan, just as he had done the morning before. But, to his surprise, Morgan had already begun reciting a verse from the text, as the book levitated across the room.

"With the passing of six long days, the Master forged the World, and breathed life into the first of its people. He called him Angel. And into him, He poured a power like the universe had never known. A piece of the Master's own essence rested within the Angel. A piece of His kindness. His benevolence. His generosity—"

The book stopped in the air just in front of Morgan, as he finished the verse.

"And His WRATH!!!"

Suddenly, Morgan summoned his wings and the book scattered into a thousand pieces. A perilous wind exploded through the room, hurling chunks of brick and debris into the air, as ripped pages fluttered about in an astonishing frenzy.

Mr. English cried out in dismay as the mere look in Morgan's eyes sent a surge of Angelic power that launched him across the room, slamming him through a wooden door.

Morgan turned toward the five royal guards and realized that they had all conjured swords into their hands, including the young Randir. Randir, who carried out the orders of his father. Ones like Order 13!

Morgan's rage released in the form of Angelic lighting, which ripped from the veins of his hands and into the chest of the man that stood between him and Randir. Sparks burst from the man's armor and, in an instant, he was on the ground.

The others tried to surround him, but Morgan summoned the fallen warrior's sword into his hand. Morgan blocked the swing of a blade just inches before it touched his eyes and smashed his wing against his attacker's face, tossing him through the air like a child's plaything.

But Morgan was unprepared for Randir, whose wings rushed out of him and blasted him with an unseen power, knocking the sword from his hand and stabbing it into the wall behind him. Randir flew at him, blowing right through the paper and debris, ready to strike the blue-haired youth.

But just before he could reach him, Randir felt a foot drilling into the back of his neck, slamming his head into the stone floor just in front of Morgan.

Morgan looked up in fear when he realized that it was Simon floating in front of him, his golden wings outstretched, a hollow ring of water spinning lethally around his two fingers. Before Morgan could take a second breath, Simon had already pitched the watery blade in his direction.

Morgan gasped. There had been no time for him to move, but the water did not touch him. He could feel a wisp of air spin past his ear as the liquid ring shot right by. Morgan had realized too late that another soldier was approaching him from behind, ready to swipe him in the back.

The ring sheered into the man's head and his face disappeared in a splash of red. Morgan turned just in time to see what he had only heard about in poems. It was the sight of a dying Angel falling to the ground and scattering into cosmic ash.

Before Morgan could even turn back, he could feel Simon's presence whipping around him, cutting a swath of silver ash through the entire room, until there was only the two of them. Morgan opened his mouth to speak, but he suddenly felt Simon's hand grab his own and was yanked off of his feet an instant later.

As their hands met, that feeling washed over him once more. That feeling of the man's essence. And it was telling him not to fear. Because he was there to take him out of that. To take him home....

STEP 2
CREATION DAY

Rising Mountain towered high above the city, as the first remnants of snowfall began to descend upon the kingdom. Very soon, the place would be blanketed in a marvelous sea of white, which stretched further than any eyes could see.

Somewhere among those thousands of tiny lights in the city, Tabitha Marcus had just finished her Creation Day decorations. She looked up at her globe—a representation of the World from the heavens—and the string of vials filled with light-oil, and smiled. With that, she waved her hand across the vials and they began to light up.

"Perfect," she said to herself, quickly stuffing all of the hand-wrapped gift boxes under the globe. She hoped to surprise her children before they returned from the marketplace with their father. And that was exactly who she expected to find when she heard a knock at her door.

But when she came to the door, she instead found one of her

neighbors, Jayson. Tiny snowflakes rushed in on a cool breeze as she held the door open for her friend.

"Jayson," Tabitha said. "This is a surprise."

"Hello, Tabitha," Jayson answered through that golden beard of his. "I just wanted to wish you and your family a Merry Creation Day."

Jayson pulled from his pocket a small green box with a red bow.

"Thank you," Tabitha laughed, accepting the gift. "This is such a surprise. I'm ashamed to admit I don't have anything for you."

"Don't trouble yourself. The Master says charity is divine, after all."

"You've been studying," Tabitha said. "I can tell."

"Yes… Goodnight."

With that, she bid the young man a farewell, and he bundled his hands into his pockets from the cold as he turned and floated down from the upstairs doorway to the streets, where Tabitha knew his home was.

But the man did not walk back into that home. Instead, he just continued walking down the street, laughing through a haze of his own breath, made visible by the winter night air. Along his way, he passed another man, who looked astonished at the sight of him. The man looked exactly like him.

As the man continued to laugh, he turned directly toward the other with a smile. But the smile suddenly stretched itself unnaturally far across his face and his entire head began to twist and contort right before his eyes. The man dropped the sack full of gifts he was carrying in horror, as he watched the creature that had once looked exactly like him suddenly take the shape of another man.

The real Jayson looked up in stunned silence as the being lifted up and glided away with twisted, flesh-covered wings.

Before Jayson could wonder why an Angel would use his gift in such a way, he was startled again by a terrible explosion of flame and debris. Jayson turned around as the ground rippled and a wave of heat rushed past him. A stream of smoke and ash had descended through the snow from just above his own house. And that was when he realized it.

"Tabitha…"

~ * ~

"I can understand your confusion. The truth is, I didn't know who you really were until long after we fought at the teahouse the other night. If I had, the situation most certainly would have turned out differently. I went to Rising Mountain to report a young Angel that had been out after curfew, thinking that you were just a thief. One with exceptional powers, yes, but a thief nonetheless. That was when I heard of King Brennan's adopted son. When I pressed the guards for information, I learned that you were scheduled to be executed, because you were too young to have wings, and the king considered you a creation of evil. No matter what the cost, I knew that I had to stop him. And so, I rescued you. Luckily, there is no one left alive that saw me… Morgan, are you listening to me?"

"What?"

Morgan lifted his head up toward the Angel carrying him through the clouds with sad eyes. Simon sighed. Of course the boy would have trouble paying attention at a time like this. His father had just disowned him for having wings, and tried to destroy him. But Simon did not know what else to say or do, other than explain what was happening, as they flew over the city, headed for his house.

At last, they arrived, and Morgan followed him in, wiping away his eyes under the illumination of the light panels on the walls. The place was small, reflecting the meager salaries the king provided for his police officers. But Morgan became intrigued when he found Simon knocking on a panel on the floor, as though it were someone's front door. He threw away the old rug that had covered it and said "I've returned."

Morgan watched curiously as the floor panel was pushed open by a woman underneath, and Simon ushered him over to join them.

"What is this?" Morgan asked.

As he drew closer to the passage, he realized that it led to a secret underground chamber, which was at least five times as large as Simon's house above.

He dropped down through the passage and looked around in bewildered fascination at all the different faces that stared back at him. Faces that belonged to merchants, and fathers, and blacksmiths, and even a few children. They were all citizens of Moralvia. But why were they hiding here, in this dank, old cave?

"You're back," a voice came out from the crowd.

Morgan turned around, to see who that enchanting voice had come from. Crimson hair framed her young face, matching the color of her eyes, which seemed almost to shimmer under the panel lights as she walked past Morgan. The moment her path crossed his, he felt a strange sensation. Something about her ensnared his attention.

"We were starting to worry," she continued.

"I am fine," Simon replied. "This is Morgan." He gestured over to Morgan, who stood slightly unsure of what to say or do. "Morgan, this is Cherry."

"So this is the one you lost so much sleep over," she said, looking at him with a smile. "His portrait in the Southern Sanctuary doesn't do him justice."

Morgan cracked a half-smile, not certain exactly what she meant, or how serious she was about it. There was not much he could think to say, so he simply let out the first thing that came to mind.

"Someone put up a painting of me in a Sanctuary?"

"Morgan," Simon said, ignoring his question. "Do you know where you are?"

Morgan blinked his eyes. There were so many things being thrown at him all at once. By the time he could ask one question, several more arose in his mind. He had barely had time to wonder about where he was before something else crept into his thoughts.

Simon continued.

"There are those, like your father, who have great power. And, among those with great power, there are some, also like your father, who feel very strongly that all those within their dominion must believe in the same things that they do. Great charity is delivered upon those that do believe. But terrible vengeance is loosed upon those that do not. My name is Simon Donnigan. And I am part of an organization that seeks to change that."

"You're members of Unity!"

Morgan took a step back. Living in the castle, he would often hear whispers of a group of rebels hiding in the kingdom, who sought only to destroy the harmony of Moralvia. All who spoke of them did so with disgust. To those in the castle, they were vermin. Fools who hated the Master and did whatever they could to keep others from believing in Him. Even killing innocent people.

"Believe me," Simon said, pushing up his glasses. "I know what your father says about Unity. But the fact that he tried to have you killed, and I was the one that prevented it, should prove to you that we are not the monsters you've been told we are."

"There's a lot we can learn," Cherry interjected. "From each other."

"Like how to turn your back on the Master?" Morgan snapped.

He could not believe what he had just said. Morgan was never very interested in the Master or the Angelic Text. But now, he suddenly found himself shouting words in defense of such things. And why?

Morgan looked up to find that Cherry was turning and walking away. Could the things he had said really have hurt her? But why would they, if she was apart of Unity? They didn't think the Master even existed. Did they?

"That wasn't very nice," Simon whispered.

"But why should she care?" Morgan asked. "She doesn't believe in the Master."

"Of course she does. But that is not the—"

Before Simon could continue, he was approached by another man, who had just entered from the passage above.

"We just received word," the man whispered into Simon's ear. "A Preacher from the North Sanctuary has been killed. A woman called Tabitha Marcus."

Morgan watched in slight surprise at the way Simon's face changed when he heard the news. It was clear that a great deal of what he had been told about Unity was wrong. No one from the Unity his father spoke of would ever weep for a dead Preacher.

"I must go," Simon said.

"Wait," Morgan let out. "Where are you going? I want to go as well."

"It isn't safe for a prince, let alone one that the king tried to execute, to walk the streets. I'm an officer of the law. And I have a job to do."

With that, Simon's golden wings flapped past Morgan's face and he was gone.

Among all those strange faces, Morgan suddenly felt very alone...

~ * ~

White sunlight poured in eerily through the charred opening in the house that had been blown out by the explosion only hours earlier. Simon stood among the last remnants of Tabitha's home. The Creation Day globe she had decorated that night was covered in black, like everything else in the room.

Footsteps of other officers clamoring for clues echoed through the hollow, lifeless den. Among them stood the proud Valan Wilstaff, apprenticed to Simon for three years, and one of his closest associates in law enforcement.

Simon felt a flicker of intuition as he knelt down toward what must have once been a doll, half-wrapped for Tabitha's daughter. His hand stopped just before touching the doll. Shirking hesitation, he finally turned the toy over on its side to find a few blackened leaves.

"Fire leaves," he said to himself.

"What?" Valan asked, approaching from behind.

Without turning, he took one of them up into his hand and held it up above him. Light shined through the holes in the leaf.

Fireleaf was used for only one purpose. They were lit up during a special prayer, at the end of each season. The flame represented the person's resolution to begin the next season with a clean slate. To start again.

But Fireleaves never left the Sanctuary. Somehow, some twisted individual had found a way to pervert the Fireleaves into a dreadful weapon, which allowed him to destroy his victims from afar. By lighting Fireleaves and leaving them with their intended target.

"This is a message," Simon said at last, as a cold chill crept through the room...

~ * ~

"Wanna help me decorate the globe?"

Morgan barely had time to rise from the poorly-made bed he had been given before Cherry was already hovering over him enthusiastically, tossing a large bundle of string with fire-oil lights into his lap.

"Uh...sure?"

"Great, let's go!"

Wiping the sleep from his eyes, Morgan was yanked out of bed and pulled across the underground chamber toward the far back wall, where the Creation Day globe sat completely bare. Morgan stared at it for a moment, realizing that he had never seen one without decorations already placed upon it, by his father's servants. The World looked so small and empty without the lights and strange shapes hanging off of it.

"Okay," Cherry said with a smile, grabbing one end of the string from the bundle in Morgan's arms. "I'll go this way and you go that way."

Morgan struggled to walk around the globe and keep from being tangled up in the string, as Cherry hung some evenly around it. It seemed that Cherry had already forgotten about the things Morgan had said to her the night before. Morgan was glad.

"It's strange," Cherry said. "I never understood what lights and funny objects had to do with Creation Day. I can understand the giving of gifts. But I can't think of a single connection between these outlandish decorations and the Master creating the World. Nor can I think of what a man in red, sneaking into your home to deliver more gifts, has to do with it either."

"Then why do you still bother to decorate the globe?"

Cherry stopped for a moment. It was a perfectly valid question.

"Well," she began, unsure of what she was going to say. "…I suppose I just think it looks pretty."

Morgan smiled. "So, where do you live?"

"Right here. My parents died a few years ago, so Simon let me live with him here. A few others as well."

Morgan listened as Cherry continued on. He was saddened to hear that Cherry's parents had been killed during a protest at the castle gates, as they were hoping to reverse the king's recent decision about taxation. And she was not the only one who had lost loved ones over what seemed like such frivolous reasons. Many of them lived there in that underground place. Others lived elsewhere in the city. Each of them with an unfortunate view of King Brennan's ways. Morgan let out a sigh. He knew firsthand that such views about his former father were more than deserved.

"I try not to think about it," Cherry said, digging into a box full of decorative ornaments. "The bad things that have happened to people. Especially in times like this. Creation Day is just two days away. And I haven't even figured out what I'm going to get you yet."

Morgan could not help but blush. He nervously grabbed an ornament and walked all the way around the other side of the globe to place it. He could hear Cherry giggling from around the corner.

~ * ~

Simon lowered his head for a bow as he approached King Brennan at the dinner table. The king barely looked at him. He just sat there, eating from that silver plate, filled with the most wondrous foods anyone could ever have seen. The food was his release from the troubles of his kingdom. And of his family.

Simon looked down at him strangely. It was an eerie feeling to know that he had just been in the castle the day before, to report a thief, and had left the castle smuggling out the king's adopted son. And no one among them knew it. But that was not his concern. He was there as an officer.

"King Brennan," he started. "I'm afraid there has been a second murder. Andrio Jarvis, from the South District. He was a Preacher with the Southern Sanctuary."

"Another Preacher?" King Brennan asked, in-between bites of fruit.

"Yes, sir. I believe there may be a connection. Whoever it is, they seem to be targeting people that teach from the Angelic Text."

The table shook under the weight of Brennan pounding his fist upon it.

"Those Unity fools. They've hatched another plot to embarrass the Master."

Simon grit his teeth in restrained anger.

"Actually, sir, there is no evidence that the killer has anything to do with Unity. The reason I came, sir, is because I would like to request the help of a Cleric. This would allow me to know exactly what happened just before the murder."

"Nonsense. You know as well as I do, Mr. Donnigan, that the powers of the Cleric are only to be used in matters that concern the Master and the teachings of the Angelic Text. To use their gifts for any other reason would be sacrilege."

"But sir—"

"Enough. I grow tired of this. I pay you to keep peace in the streets and enforce my word among the commoners. Earn your pay and find who is doing this. Now leave me."

"Yes, my king…"

Simon turned around with a grimace. It was clear that however he was going to solve these crimes, he would have to do it alone. And it had to be quick. What little good reputation Unity had left was being expunged. And he refused to allow any more innocents to be lost.

~ * ~

Simon breathed deeply of the burning paperleaf in his hand, but it gave him no sense of calm as he had hoped it would. Through the veil of smoke, he dropped the city map and it unraveled across the table in the old library. His eyes searched the aged markings of the document for any clue as to how or why the two victims had been chosen, but arrived at little inspiration. Until he made a realization.

The top of the map represented the Northern District. The first victim had been the leading Preacher at the Sanctuary in that area. The second victim had lead the Southern Sanctuary. Only three other Sanctuaries remained in the city. The Tower of Light, which rested in the center of the city, as the shining beacon of faith in the Master's glory, and the two Sanctuaries directly east and west of it, on opposite ends.

No doubt lingered in his heart now. If more victims were to be claimed, they would have to be from one of those three locations. Simon extinguished his paperleaf and rushed out of the library.

~ * ~

Morgan began to grow weary, as he followed Cherry around that cramped, old cave, waiting for what felt like an eternity for Simon to return. Each time he saw someone enter through the secret hatch, he jumped up, hoping it would be him. But it never was. And so, he continued to follow Cherry, as she continued with her relentless celebration of Creation Day. The anniversary of the Master's creation of the World.

With a basket full of hand-wrapped candy, she walked through the cave, handing treats out to everyone she saw. Morgan grinned at the sight of the three young children, who jumped at the chance to have some sweets. Cherry greeted everyone with a warm smile and a "Merry Creation Day."

But Morgan grew impatient. His mind wandered, as it often did, and so did his feet. He found himself listening to the men at the table in the corner of the room, his attention drifting further and further from wherever Cherry was headed next.

At the head of the table sat the large and brutish Aganon, who shook the whole table with a mere gesture.

"I am growing tired of hiding in holes," Aganon began, "while the king and his court live lavishly, plotting the ruination of our lives as they sit on their feather pillows and sip wine. I want change!"

"We all do," a woman responded. "But every time we pick up weapons, we become more like they are. Those fools who think they can change people by driving swords into their gut."

"Well, what would you have us do? Stay here and plan another 'peaceful demonstration'? Another protest? And watch as the king's soldiers come and drag half of our friends away in the process? That will do nothing!"

"Merry Creation Day!"

Morgan squinted uncomfortably as Cherry's hand, filled with candy treats, darted over toward Aganon's face. It was as if the poor girl had no idea that she had just interrupted a serious, tense discussion, between men and women who seemed quite angry. It did not seem to matter to her. She was there to wish them all a Merry Creation Day, and to give them the candy that she had worked all morning to make herself.

"Do not speak those words to me!" Aganon shouted, turning away from the girl.

"Hey there!" Morgan spoke, stepping in front of Cherry, to her surprise. "Why did you do that? She only wanted to wish you a Merry—"

"I do not partake in your holiday, and I refuse to listen to those words. They are offensive to me."

"But why? All she wanted to—"

"Morgan," Cherry interrupted.

Before Morgan could respond any further, Cherry had quickly dropped a few candies on the table and pulled him away from everyone.

"It's alright," Cherry said.

"What do you mean it's alright?" Morgan asked, irritated by that mannerless man.

"I forgot he didn't believe in the Text. I should not have said that to him."

Morgan did not understand. From his view, Cherry had done nothing wrong, and that boorish man should have apologized. But Cherry saw it completely differently. She was sorry that her words, which were entirely pure in intention, had offended the man. Because he had no faith in the Master.

"I thought you people believed in the Master," Morgan said frankly.

"We people," Cherry responded, slightly annoyed, "are not all the same. Unity's members believe many different things. That is what separates us from King Brennan and his court. We choose the things we put our faith into. They believe that they should choose it for us."

With that, Cherry turned and continued handing out candy, as though nothing had happened. Morgan stood there, still perplexed at what had just transpired. And in all this time, he still wondered where Simon was, and what it was that he had sensed from him back at the castle…

~ * ~

Simon buttoned up his black coat as it flapped in the winter breeze. As he flew over the city, his eyes scanned the rooftops of the West District, searching for the next house on his list. At last, he descended from the sky and landed on the street designated in his list.

Just a few houses from where he stood was the home of Danius Grimm, the youngest Preacher ever to lead any Sanctuary. He was only 20 years old, and already teaching the Text to children less than half his own age, as well as their parents and families. Simon hoped that he might be able to ask him if he had seen anyone suspicious recently, or at the very least, warn him of the crimes being committed against his colleagues.

As Simon approached the entrance to the house, he stood there for a moment, his hand frozen in the air, as he hesitated to knock. A strange feeling had fallen over him, but it was an uncertain one. Before he could shrug it away, the door opened on its own as he realized someone was leaving the house.

"You are most welcome," a man spoke. His long, raven-colored hair was all that he could see, since his back was turned, as he bade farewell to whoever was inside and quickly walked out of the doorway.

"Hello," Simon said, wondering if this might be Danius Grimm. But as the man walked by, he felt a powerful presence. For a fraction of an instant, a cloud of restrained rage seemed to pass along with him. The man did not answer. He simply kept walking.

Simon turned with urgency in his eyes as he realized that the young man inside the house, saying "goodbye" to the one that had just left, was Danius Grimm. And he was holding the small, green box that had just been given to him by the man quickly walking away.

"May I help you?" Danius asked, confused.

But before Danius could move, Simon had already burst through his doorway, frantically snatching the box from his hand. With all his strength, Simon hurled the box through the doorway and tackled a dumfounded Danius to the floor.

The tiny box darted through the air for only a moment, before the fireleaves packed within began to ignite, and the box exploded. Danius shouted out in astonishment as he watched the windows of his house all shatter and waves of smoke rushed into the room. He looked up, expecting to see the officer that had saved his life, but by the time his eyes caught up with him, he was merely a shadow, dashing out of the house and into that horrible cloud of blackness.

Simon's wings ejected out of his back as he emerged from the cloak of ash that loitered in the air, cutting across the sky as quickly as he could to find that raven-haired man that had just left. There was no doubt anymore. That power he had sensed. It was one he had felt once before.

Simon whipped through the air between buildings, following the trail of energy he struggled to keep ahold of. But suddenly, he felt the man's foot ram into his back, forcing him out of the sky. Simon turned in the air just before he felt a hand latch around his neck. With a loud crash, Simon slammed onto the roof of an old building, pinned down by more hands than could possibly have belonged to one person.

But it *was* only one person. And those four or five hands had sprouted out of his terrible, twisted body in grotesque, unimaginable ways. The creature's hair hung around him like a hood. His face was jumbled, but close enough to what he remembered to know that it was him.

"Kraven," Simon let out hoarsely.

Simon grit his teeth in disgust. He had hoped never to see his face again. The face of a man that had once been apart of Unity, but one day disappeared and did not return, until that day, nearly two years later. And no one among them had missed his presence. For he had used his Angelic gift, the power to change his shape, in the most violent ways imaginable. His ways were not their ways. And Simon was relieved to have been rid of him.

"I'm glad you still remember me," Kraven said as he gripped his neck with inhuman fingers. His voice was a constant ghostlike whisper. "I had hoped one of you would recognize your old friend's handiwork before the job was finished."

"This is not what we wanted," Simon pleaded.

"Isn't it? When my task is complete, and those fat, self-serving fools are all dead, the city will be free to live as it pleases. I think that this is exactly what we wanted. You just don't have the stomach to make it happen."

"You're wrong," Simon said.

It was clear, by the look in Kraven's ever-changing eyes, that there was no reasoning with him. And so, as Simon continued, he slowly began to activate his powers, gathering up the moisture in the air for an attack.

"Unity's path is not meant to be so bloody. That is not what we stand for."

Simon struggled to pull together enough water to form a weapon behind Kraven's back, but it was not to be. Kraven curled his lips into a giant smile, and smashed Simon's head against the roof. A splash of water could be heard as his power over the water failed him.

Kraven raised a fist and an assortment of bones pushed their way through the flesh of his knuckles.

"I do not care to harm you, Simon. But if you stand in my way again, I will not be as forgiving as the Master would."

Kraven swiftly punched Simon in the face and hurled himself into the air, the sound of bones popping in and out of place chattering on the wind as he disappeared into the approaching night. Simon raised a hand to stop him, but it was far too late. His hand dropped as his injuries forced him into a nightmarish slumber…

~ * ~

"Do you miss him?"

Morgan's spoon nearly dropped into the bowl of soup in front of him. He looked over to the other side of his bed, where Cherry sat there, sipping her soup, waiting for an answer. It was the last thing he was expecting her to ask.

"King Brennan?" Morgan asked. "Why would I miss him?"

"Well," Cherry started. "I know he is your adopted father, and he did many mean things to you. But he is still your father. Or the closest thing you have had."

For some reason that Morgan did not understand, the thought of Simon dashed through his thoughts.

"I don't need a father," Morgan said. "I'm not a child."

"You're only a year younger than I am," Cherry insisted. "But I still think of myself as a child."

Morgan stared at her. He felt no reason to respond to that at all.

"If I still had a father, I think I'd miss him. Even if he did bad things sometimes."

Just then, a loud clatter sounded. Cherry nearly dropped her bowl of soup in surprise. Morgan looked up toward the secret hatch in the ceiling. He had done it countless times in the last few days, hoping that it would be Simon that came through. But this time, a terrible feeling crept into his heart, and he wished that it would be anyone else.

Morgan leapt to his feet at the sight of him. It was Simon, barely conscious, in the arms of a man that quickly carried him inside. An arm rushed across an old table, clearing it of mugs and bowls, as he was gently placed onto it. A crowd gathered, shouting frightening things like "death" and "killer." Morgan pushed through to see that his face was bruised, his lip stained with redness.

"What could have done this?" one man asked.

"Kraven," Simon forced out, as his eyelids fluttered unevenly.

People gasped.

"That lunatic has gone too far. He must be stopped."

"But what about Simon?" Cherry asked. No one seemed to pay any attention to her.

Morgan turned and realized that Aganon was stomping over toward the table with an angry look through his thick moustache. Morgan immediately curled his hand into a fist. He did not want that boorish peasant to come anywhere near him.

"Leave him alone," Morgan said.

But Aganon paid no heed to the young prince. From the

opposite side of the table, he raised a rough, calloused hand into the air. Morgan's eyes widened in fear over what the giant brute might do. But suddenly, a pair of pure, white wings extended from Aganon's back, and a great rush of warmth permeated the air. Aganon waved his hand over Simon's body and a white energy passed over him, healing his wounds.

"I see," Aganon said. "The injury was not as bad as it looked. If it was, you would not be able to rise so quickly."

And so, Simon did rise. He silently shook the man's massive hand, paying thanks for the help of his gift once more.

"Ready to go?" Aganon asked.

"Go?" Morgan interrupted. "Go where?"

"I have to stop Kraven from finishing his plan," Simon answered. "It is not only Preachers who are at stake, but Unity itself, in the eyes of the people."

"We will not fail," Aganon said. "Will we?"

Three other men stepped forward in response, ready to join Simon in his search. They were the three friends, Galvin, Orlo, and Hadar. For many years, Orlo had served Unity alongside the two brown-winged brothers, Galvin and Hadar Ackson, having faced many dangers together, but few as great as the one they sought now.

Orlo quickly spoke, as he stowed a sword into a pocket of invisible air.

"Two more victims have been claimed since yesterday. That leaves only the Tower of Light. The Preacher lives in the tower itself. There is no time to waste."

Simon began to walk out, hoping that the others did not sense that he was still slightly injured. But Morgan stepped forth to stop him.

"I'm going with you," he claimed.

"I'm afraid not," Simon retorted. "You are too important to be lost in such trivial matters."

"Trivial?!"

Morgan was offended. He knew that he was a prince, but there was no way that he could ever bring himself to look upon heartless killings as a trivial event.

But it was too late. Simon and the others had already left, leaving him yet again. To wait. And wonder.

"I'm sorry, Morgan," Cherry said. "He only wants to keep you safe."

Morgan turned to her with anger in his eyes. His father had tried to execute him, he had been smuggled out of his home, ripped away from all that he had known, and forced to sit in that dreadful cave for days without any answers. What Cherry had said to him sounded positively absurd!

"Safe?" Morgan shouted. "I'm not a child!"

"I know! But you are…"

"Are what?"

Cherry took a deep breath.

"Book 13 of the Angelic Text talks about a new generation of Angels. A generation of Angels that are blessed with wings from birth. Angels that will one day bring the Master back to the World. And the Angels will walk alongside the Master once again, as it was in the Beginning. These Angels are called the Alorium... Simon believes that you are one of them. Maybe even the first."

Morgan looked around at a room filled with faces all staring down at him, much like as it was when he first had entered that cave. But now he understood more clearly why so many of them had such a fascination with him. This was what his father had spoken of so many days earlier, with such distain. The Alorium. But this was not a part of any version of the text that he knew of.

"There is no Book 13," Morgan finally said. "The Text ends with Book 12. Believe me, I know. The worst teacher in all of Moralvia hammered it into my mind since I was four years old."

"Actually," Cherry said, "there are 14 Books, but that is not important now. Simon wanted you to stay here, because he believes that you are Alorium. And, if you were to die, you may be the only one there ever is..."

~ * ~

The Tower of Light shimmered brightly under the glow of the moons that hung in the sky above. It was the highest point in the entire city, excluding Rising Mountain. Constructed of luminous stone from an ancient cave that gave off a gold shimmer when touched by moonlight. But the moons were quickly being covered by layers of thick clouds, which marched across the sky, ready to release one final night's worth of snow before the dawn of Creation Day, which was only a few hours away.

Simon and his four friends rushed through the air in a line, which quickly scattered as they approached the tower, circling the area, searching for any suspicious entities.

Orlo landed at the top of the tower, hoping to gain the greatest view of the district below. But he suddenly realized that what he had landed on was not the roof of the tower at all. He looked down to find that a vicious claw had somehow emerged from below and locked around his neck. Orlo cried out for help, but by then, he could already feel Kraven's shape-shifting arms slithering all around him like snakes. Orlo tried to summon his wings, but was barely able to move. Kraven's body had almost completely consumed him. The last thing he saw before total blackness was Kraven's distorted face ascending before him.

In moments, Orlo's lifeless body dropped from the roof and Kraven reconstituted his Angel form (or at least an approximation of such) and flew laughing into the night.

But suddenly, Kraven felt a strange hint of power. Simon's elbow cracked down into his back, sending him crashing down onto the roof of a nearby building.

"I owed you that!" Simon shouted, dropping out of the sky as snow began to fall over the city.

Kraven spun back up into the air, barely able to block Simon's sword with a layer of sharp bone from his arm. Sparks burst forth from the collision.

"You're a fool, Simon," Kraven yelled, effortlessly holding back the officer's blade. "I could have helped you. All of you."

"Your kind of help," Simon exclaimed, "is not something any of us needs!"

Kraven struck Simon with three bone-hardened fists, hurling him through the air at unearthly speeds. But an enraged Simon spun himself around, springing himself off of the wall of a building, and dashing right back toward his enemy.

Back at the tower, Aganon turned just in time to see as Kraven and Simon flew toward each other with bone-chilling battlecries. Even from so far, Aganon could feel a swell of power from his comrade, ready to pool all his vengeance into one final blow.

The two warriors collided, and Aganon was blinded by the explosion of Angelic power that rippled across the sky.

Simon dropped out of the air, slamming down into the snow-covered street at the entrance to the tower, steam rising from his tattered clothes. He gripped an awful wound at his side, wheezing in disbelief. How could he be that powerful?

Simon found Aganon at his side, struggling to heal him, but with little success. His gift was already exhausted, Simon's injuries so severe. The sound of Hadar and Galvin trying and failing to defeat Kraven rang out in the air. His ultimate attack had barely phased that monster.

"It's almost time," Kraven's vaporous voice echoed in the night, as he slowly landed from across the street, his beastly wings outstretched like a banner of wrath. "I have a Creation Day gift for you. I hope you like it."

Aganon looked up with angry eyes, summoning a sword into his hand. Snow crunched under his feet as he stomped his way across the street, ready to strike the creature standing there with that awful grin. But, within the time that Aganon could blink his eyes, Kraven's fist was already at his face.

Simon looked up to see his friend's broken body crashing into the ground next to him. And though he was too weak to turn and see it, he could hear Kraven's footsteps draw closer to them, as snow fell over the streets.

Kraven let out a sinister laugh as he stretched out an arm to reach down and choke the life out of his former colleague.

"Merry Creation Day," he whispered.

"STOP!"

Simon's eyes widened. Could that voice really have belonged to whom it sounded like?

Kraven recalled his arm in irritation, looking up into the sky, from which the voice had come. And up, through the sheets of snow falling from the heavens, he could see the faint image of a young man, standing at the roof of the tower. A flicker of power emanated from his blue wings as they extended around him. It was Morgan Craft.

"How sweet," Kraven laughed at Simon, still writhing at his feet. "You brought me a gift as well."

"No, wait!" Simon yelled.

It was too late. Kraven leapt up into the air and took flight, shooting up toward the blue-haired boy with beastly delight.

But, before Kraven had time to reach the top of the tower, Morgan dove straight down toward him. Kraven cried out in astonishment as he felt Morgan's foot drill into his face, sending him rocketing out of the sky, slamming through the roof of the old library, crushing a table beneath him before hitting the floor.

Simon gasped. Morgan could not have known that this would not be enough to defeat Kraven. But, to his surprise, Morgan did not stop there. Simon's glasses were thrown from his face as a blue streak shot across the sky and rammed through the library door. Clamoring echoed from the old building as chunks of stone and debris burst out of the structure, the result of a furious cosmic power tearing through the place, and rippling its way out into the surrounding street.

The doorway flew apart as Morgan's body was thrown from the library, out into the open, but he stopped himself in the air, as heavy snow continued to fall. Blood trickled from his mouth. His shirt slashed. Kraven stepped out with a bruise across his face from Morgan's kick.

"You're strong," Kraven said with a dark grin. "But I'm stronger."

"Doubtful," Morgan said, defiantly.

Kraven began to march over toward Morgan, fearlessly. But he suddenly stopped when he realized that a faint light was beginning to emerge from the tower. It seemed impossible. There were no moons to illuminate the stone. So why would the Tower of Light—this Sanctuary of rock—suddenly begin to glow?

The light intensified now, so that it seemed to flow out from just behind Morgan's back, as his wings spread out around him. The falling snow suddenly seemed to stop itself in mid-air. Kraven snarled as he could sense it—a sudden outpouring of

Angelic power, the likes of which he had never felt in his life. Flakes of snow hung weightlessly in the winter air as Morgan's eyes glistened with blue energy.

Angelic lightning crackled between the young Angel's fingers, as his hand began to tremble, barely able to contain the power struggling to break free of his grip. Kraven let out a guttural cry as he forced himself to charge toward Morgan with all the strength he could command. He soared over to him with a sword-like bone in his arm, ready to strike, but it would never reach the blue-haired boy.

Morgan threw up a hand and unleashed a snake of lightning from his grasp, which blasted Kraven with such force that it tossed him back across the street, through the frozen cloak of floating snow, right through the wall of the library. Morgan turned his back on the building just before it completely collapsed into a cloud of debris behind him and the snow finally began to fall again.

Simon watched in surprise as the young man walked over to him, the light of the tower flowing over him and his wings, as he reached down to help him. The moment Simon touched his hand, he could feel his essence. And it was telling him that he was here to help. And he was going to take him home…

STEP 3
REVELATION

A great mass of clouds marched across the heavens, glowing under the light of the morning sun, as the last remnants of snow fell upon the city. The boots of the Royal Guards sloshed through sheets of white as they searched outside the Tower of Light.

What remained of the old library, having collapsed sometime the night before, sat under a blanket of snow. It was Creation Day morning. And, as the men continued to seek clues as to who could have done this, they all wished that they could be anywhere but where they were.

Among those men stood Sirio Nichols, son of the king's oldest friend, Kaster. Long had it been since he had seen his father, who had set out on a quest to find a great treasure for the king, and did not return. For seventeen years, he waited for his homecoming, serving King Brennan in his place, as he knew his father would want.

Sirio stood atop the pile of rubble that once was the library outside the Sanctuary, his eyes scanning the area for any hint of evidence about who might have done such a thing. Suddenly, he felt a strange flash of intuition, and as he turned his head, the feeling grew even more intense.

The soldier's eyes widened as he drew his sword. Only three paces away from where he stood, a gangly set of fingers began to reach up through the broken wood and snow.

~ * ~

A green glow flowing from the light panels reflected in King Brennan's eyes as he marched down the halls of the castle, accompanied by his two personal guards, as well as Sirio Nichols. His thoughts dwelled on the events of the past several days, barely paying attention to the words of those that spoke to him, as they headed for the castle entrance.

"He was found this morning, as investigators were looking through the rubble."

"It is hard to believe that anyone could survive the collapse of an entire building."

"His gift gives him a remarkable resistance to injury."

"We thought it best for him to be brought here, since we now believe that he was working as an operative for Unity."

The giant doors to the castle slammed shut behind them as a group of Royal Guardians in red and black armor pushed their prisoner into the room. King Brennan looked across the room at the man with disgust. His neck and wrists shackled, the man showed no respect, or fear, from the king in his home. Nor would Brennan expect any from a member of Unity.

"Hello, my king," Kraven said with a devilish grin. "How did you like my Creation Day gift? I wasn't allowed to finish the festivities in time, but it was still quite a gift, if I do say so myself."

"Silence!" shouted one of the guards.

Kraven's left eye twisted around unnaturally toward the guard, who had conjured a battle-axe right to his throat.

"I will offer you one last chance to repent of your misdeeds," Brennan spoke. "…Tell me where your comrades in Unity are hiding. And any…others who might have been taken by them."

Kraven could not help but let out a laugh, in that ghostly whisper of his. How delightful, he thought, that they believed him to be in league with those that sought to stop him from destroying them all. The guard did not take kindly to his insolence, and tightened the blade around his neck. His last mistake…

Suddenly, the guard felt a wisp of air shoot past his arm, and the axe was yanked out of his grasp by a third hand, which sprouted out from Kraven's body and slashed him with his own weapon. Sparks ejected from the man's armor as he spun lifelessly to the ground. In an explosion of power, Kraven's ever-transforming body whirled around him, tossing the other guards away like trash. His terrible laugh filled the chamber as he leapt up toward the king.

But Brennan showed no fear, as the creature rushed toward him, brandishing an axe, ready to strike him down. Suddenly, Brennan summoned his black wings and an overpowering force was unleashed upon the room, which hurled Kraven's body back through the air, slamming him against the castle doors and pinning him there above the floor.

Sirio and the other guards took a step away from their king, overwhelmed by the sheer magnitude of power emanating from his body. Those pitch-black wings stretched out further and further until soon the entire room was filled with utter darkness, like night itself had come alive and wrapped itself around the castle walls.

Kraven looked out into the emptiness and, for the first time, knew true fear. He tried to pull himself away from the doors, but an imponderable force held him there, no matter what awful form he molded himself into. Then, through the unending curtains of shadow, a dark figure emerged. The glow of his hollow, white eyes lit his face.

"Kraven," King Brennan spoke. "You are a shape-changer. You have the ability to fold your wounds, so that you may survive some of the most deadly injuries… But not all."

Kraven tried to scream, but it was as if the very air he breathed was being snatched away from him, as he could feel a great dagger of energy pierce his body. In moments, his insides had begun to vaporize into particles of silver, until there was nothing left of him.

Brennan's guards gasped for air as the veil of shadows was lifted from over them, and the king's wings vanished into his back once more. When they opened their eyes, the creature known as Kraven was no more. The sound of Brennan's footsteps echoed through the chamber as he stomped imposingly out of the room, leaving Sirio to catch his breath from what he had just witnessed…

Down the hall Brennan walked, servants bowing as he passed. But Brennan made an abrupt pause as he was about to pass a nearby window. A vast sky opened up before him as he stepped closer to the window, looking out upon the grassy slopes of Rising Mountain, and a shining city below.

But something further away stirred his heart. Through the blanket of thick clouds rolling in the distance beyond the city, he could feel a presence. He did not know how or why, but a great sense of dread crept over him. Something terrible was about to visit his kingdom…

"My king."

The voice darted through the silence, recalling the king to his duties. Brennan took one last glance out the window and walked off toward his servant.

"Where is the Cleric I requested?" King Brennan spoke, before his servant had time to address him. The man cleared his throat in hesitation as he walked through the halls at his king's side.

"Yes, sire," he replied. "The Cleric is ready to perform the ceremony at any time, of course. But he had hoped that it could wait until after the morning meal."

"Very well," Brennan answered.

"I am afraid there has been another protest," the man said at last, returning to the issue at hand.

"Unity again?" Brennan asked.

"Actually, sire, I do not believe so. They appear to be ordinary citizens."

Brennan grimaced. The troubles of his kingdom extended far beyond those traitorous rebels. Now, it seemed, every man, woman, and child in Moralvia sought to question every last order he sent down.

"What is it this time?" the king inquired.

"Well… They wish to have the symbology changed on the city's gold coins."

"What?"

"They hope to have the engravings removed. The ones that say 'By the Master's Grace.' They seem to think that this sends the wrong message to those that do not share the same faith in the Master that we do."

"Nonsense. The faces of our coins have been this way since the dawn of the kingdom, and will remain as such until the World splits in two."

"As you wish," the man said, quietly.

Though he did not allow his servant to see it, Brennan could detect a sense of sadness in the man's voice. He was a loyal servant of the king's court. Did this man, whose name Brennan was ashamed never to have learned, really care so much for the folly of a few dissenting voices in the city?

Brennan pushed away his concerns as they entered the dining hall, and the man took his leave.

All across the long dining table, a lavish display of various foods awaited him. And, on either side of the king's chair, sat many members of the Sanctuary, as well as Mr. English, who sat near to his left. Their guest that morning was Sirio Nichols. It was his reward for discovering Kraven. To dine in the presence of noblekind.

"Apologies for being late," Brennan said, as he took his seat.

"My king," Mr. English whispered. "Perhaps it would be better for you to put that away."

Brennan looked down to see that the teacher was gesturing toward the blue amulet around his neck. He did not even realize that it had fallen outside of his clothing. He quickly grabbed it to place it back behind his shirt. But the moment he did, he felt a strange twinge of power. Not often did he invoke the amulet's gifts, but this time, it felt as though the amulet had invoked him instead. But what was it that he sensed?

Sirio looked over in confusion at the king's face. Something about the jewel around his neck seemed familiar to him, but he could not remember where he might have seen it, or why he felt so strangely upon seeing it around the king's neck. He shrugged away the feelings as a conversation began.

"So," one of the Clerics asked. "How goes the pursuit of those Unity traitors?"

"It goes well," Brennan answered flatly, as he broke a roll of bread in his hands.

"And what did you do with those that were captured?" asked another.

"Come now," Mr. English interjected. "We all know the

penalties for such betrayal. There is no need to interrupt this blessed meal with such unpleasant business."

"I agree," Brennan said with a heavy breath.

Mr. English sighed quietly as he took up a glass of spring water. After Brennan had flown into a rage at him two days earlier, for simply mentioning Morgan in his presence, he knew not to upset the king by bringing up unhappy memories. But through the false smiles and pleasant greetings, Brennan knew that an unhealthy desire to see the child destroyed rested with him. That child, which the Angelic Text—at least the version he had devoted his life to—called an abomination.

Brennan sipped his Hangman's Tea, and held the glass up before him. A memory drifted into his thoughts. This was the tea that Morgan had begged him to let him try, three years ago. Brennan suddenly let out a laugh, remembering the foolishness that had ensued that night, as he struggled to keep the boy from drinking it, for it would have made him quite drunk.

The rest of the room turned to their king in confusion. No one seemed to know what was so amusing. Nor could they ever....

~ * ~

King Brennan stood there staring at the empty chamber for what seemed like hours. His two guards were confused. Why were they simply standing there for so long, in this place where his son had somehow escaped execution? The man let out a sigh.

Finally, through the doorway, a man in a pure white uniform

with a black collar entered the room. In his hand, he held the Angelic Text. He was a Cleric of the Sanctuary.

"Thank you for coming," Brennan said, quietly. It was the most gentle his voice had ever been in public view.

"Thank you," the Cleric replied. "For gracing me with the presence of such a noble servant of the Master."

"I trust you've been told of my request."

The man nodded with a kind smile. "Please, give me room."

Brennan waved off his guards as the three of them stepped back behind him, near the only door. From there, they watched as a pair of grey wings rose from him, covered in strange markings in black. Markings that belonged to a generation that had long since passed. The Cleric raised his hands and began to speak the words of an ancient tongue. The sacred language of the Sanctuary, passed down from the original text, written so long ago.

His words flowed through the air, awakening some sleeping essence that rested in the room. The pace of Brennan's heart began to quicken within him as he could feel a great surge of life sweep through the place. In moments, he and his guards were enchanted by the sight of particles of silver Angelic ash beginning to collect within the room. Those tiny points of light gathered and formed into the faint image of those soldiers that had perished in the chamber only a few days earlier.

But they were not complete. The Cleric began to sweat, as he struggled to hold their shapes together. In the center of the room, with only half a face, and one arm, the phantom form of Royal

Guardian Randir slowly turned up onto what remained of his back. King Brennan rushed over to his side, wide-eyed at what he saw. The great Randir, or at least what little of his essence the Cleric could gather, lying on the ground before him, after having been slain.

"Randir," Brennan whispered. "Who was it? Who did this to you?...What happened to my son?"

Randir struggled to force breath from lungs that were barely there.

"S-Si...mon.... Donnigan...."

"The police man?" Brennan asked in confusion. "What does he have to do with this?"

'My k-king.... My ki..."

Randir frantically grabbed Brennan's arm with his only hand. Startled, Brennan knew not what to do, but he struggled to hold him in his arms, perhaps to comfort him. But it was impossible. Brennan looked down in horror as the last remnants of Randir suddenly dropped back into cosmic ash. Whatever remained of him trickled down through his fingers and vanished.

The guards rushed to help the Cleric as he nearly fell over, unable to hold their essence any longer. They looked at his king, crouched down, his back turned to them as he stared at the empty space on the floor before him.

"Find that police man...."

STEP 4
CONFESSION

Morgan smiled as he watched a snowflake fall into the palm of his hand. It was the first time in so long that he could enjoy the season, if only for a moment. Cherry kindly grabbed the hood from behind him and pulled it over his head for him, to keep away the cold, as well as to keep him unseen. Long had it been since Morgan was awake so early, even if it was Creation Day morning.

Hadar Ackson let out a sigh as he flashed a look of annoyance to his brother, Galvin. He had no desire to do as he was asked, but as a favor to Simon, the man that had invited them into Unity many years ago, he and Galvin had agreed.

"Where are we going?" Morgan asked, curiously, as they stepped off of the porch at Simon's house.

"Has the good king not taught you the meaning of patience, Your Majesty?" Hadar asked, sarcastically.

It was clear to Morgan that Hadar, like many, was not among

those that cared for his former father. But Galvin gave a silent frown to his younger brother, and silenced him.

"You must forgive my brother," Galvin said. "We are going to the Southern Sanctuary."

"But why not visit the Tower of Light?" Morgan asked in confusion. "Is it not closer?"

"Yes," Galvin replied. "But there is someone in particular Simon would like you to meet. A Preacher from the Southern District."

Morgan groaned. Living on Rising Mountain, all he ever wanted to do was to visit the city, to explore all those things that he never had the chance to see in the company of his father. And now that he was no longer a resident of the castle, he was being carted back to speak to a Preacher of the Angelic Text, which was hammered into his thoughts for years as a child.

"Come," Hadar said, impatiently.

Galvin and Hadar both held out their hands for the two youths to grab ahold of them. Morgan watched Cherry take Hadar's hand without hesitation. The moment Morgan's hand touched Galvin's, he felt a pulse of Angelic power course between them. In an instant, the four of them had lifted into the air, Cherry and Morgan being pulled along as their two guardians flew high above the streets on brown-feathered wings.

Morgan felt strange, being led through the air under another Angel's power, knowing that he was perfectly capable of flying on his own. But because of that foolish belief that so many shared, he was unable to fly freely during the day, for fear that someone may see him—a child, with wings. Morgan made certain to keep the hood low over his face, so as to keep his identity hidden from any below that may see him.

As the wind rushed past them, Morgan could feel a hint of Galvin's essence in his hand. Hadar had many reservations about Simon's wishes on that day, but it was clear that Galvin did not share those feelings. Morgan's eyes widened. Did Galvin really believe he was that special?

The last traces of snow fell around them as they passed over the Tower of Light. Morgan looked down, realizing that there were a number of Royal Guardians scattered about the streets, doubtlessly searching for clues as to who might have caused the collapse of the old library.

Morgan closed his eyes in distress. The weight of his situation had grown heavy on his heart, as they snuck around the city with people that plotted the ruination of the king's court. But why should he care, he wondered, when this man had tried to destroy him?

Morgan opened his eyes to the feeling of Cherry's touch into his free hand, as a cool breeze swept through her crimson hair.

~ * ~

"Are you listening?"

Simon pushed up his glasses as he turned toward his old trainee, Valan Wilstaff. He tried his best to shirk the haunting memories of what he had witnessed the night before—those astonishing things that Morgan had done, and what may lie ahead for them. It grew more and more difficult to focus on their assigned task on that morning, as he wished he was able to join Morgan on that day, of all days.

But his duty as an officer demanded his attention, and he could not ignore that obligation.

"I'm sorry, Valan," Simon said. "You found another one?"

Valan silently gestured toward the wall in the alleyway. Scrawled across the wall was a crude painting. The same painting that had begun to appear all over the city, on various buildings and monuments across Moralvia. It was the face of Danver Algus, the man rumored to have destroyed the Craftian Statue nearly 70 years ago.

Simon's eyes narrowed behind his glasses. The Craftian Statue, modeled after the grandfather of the king, had been erected in his honor, a shining beacon of his kingdom's faith in the Master. When Danver Algus had been captured, he claimed that the destruction of the statue was a symbol of the end of the old ways, when brown-winged Angels were forced into servitude and forbidden to have jobs or own property. The loss of the monument ended a dark chapter in the history of their society. But now the image of Danver Algus was appearing all over the city, calling the entire kingdom's ways into question. And King Brennan wanted the defacements to end.

"Unity scum."

Simon turned away from the words of his trainee, biting back his aggravation.

"They are fools," Valan continued. "Defacing the city, seeking to drag the rest of us into the pit of faithlessness along with them."

"Valan," Simon said at last. "There is no reason to believe this was done by Unity. I do no believe they would care to do such a thing."

"Of course they would," Valan insisted. "They display the face of a criminal to incite more criminal activity, and have their own crimes validated in the eyes of the people. They are without faith. Without morality. And they must be wiped out."

Valan was startled to see Simon immediately leap into the air, his golden wings outspread, disappearing behind a tall building. He stood there, confused. Why, he thought, would a noble officer such as Simon be concerned with common criminals?

~ * ~

Cherry sat at the back of the room, marveling at the beautiful stained glass ceiling of the Sanctuary, waiting with the others for the Preacher to finish bidding farewell to his visitors. Creation Day morning services had just ended.

When Cherry turned to her right, she found that Morgan was staring toward the front of the room in fascination.

Behind the altar, where the Preacher stood in his black uniform, was a great painting. Just as Cherry had mentioned only a few nights before, there was a portrait of Morgan hanging, nearly as tall as the wall itself.

The painting depicted Morgan in the princely clothes that he had all but forgotten about, standing in a commanding pose. He looked strong. Fearless. He looked like the future ruler of Moralvia.

Morgan did not think it looked anything like him.

But as the last few visitors finally began to leave, the Preacher approached with a smile.

"The Ackson Brothers," the man spoke, recognizing the two. "It has been far too long. I trust you are still keeping up with your studies." He raised his copy of the Angelic Text with a smile.

"Oh, of course," Hadar answered, falsely.

"We…have a guest," Galvin said. "The one Simon spoke with you about. Morgan Craft, please meet Reverend Foster Drake."

Morgan was unprepared for the look of admiration that was about to befall the man's face when he realized who it was that was sitting before him. He bowed his head in respect. But it was not because of his royal status.

"Alorium," the man said softly. "It is an honor."

Morgan was accustomed to the bowing of heads, but never in such a fashion, and with an uncomfortable crack in his voice, he stood up.

"N-Not at all," he tried to laugh. "I…I'm pleased to meet you."

"Well," Hadar said, flatly. "You must have much to talk about. We will return shortly."

An annoyed Galvin watched his impertinent brother walk out as quickly as his legs could carry him, eager to be out of that place. Galvin gave a friendly nod to follow him out.

"I'd like to stay a while, if you don't mind," Cherry asked. "I have not been to Sanctuary in some time."

Morgan smiled silently to himself. At least he would have one person nearby while he dealt with uneasy business.

~ * ~

"Halt!"

Simon turned to find that Valan had darted out of the air toward the street below, his red wings extended. He had seen someone standing before the wall of a house, where a painting had just been scribbled.

Simon rushed down after them. As good as Valan's intentions might have been, he knew that he could not allow him to catch the culprit on his own.

A figure in a black cloak ran through the streets, into the tunnel beneath a bridge, beyond the sight of the two flying officers, sprinting away as quickly as it could. As Valan flew down toward the first entrance to the tunnel, Simon sped toward the opposite side.

A wet paintbrush dropped to the ground as the cloaked suspect rushed to the tunnel's exit, hoping desperately to stay ahead of its pursuers. But just as the figure emerged through the arch of the tunnel, a pair of hands shot down and yanked it up into the air.

A frenzy of wind whipped past the suspect as he felt himself be tossed up and onto the deck of the bridge above. Simon's boots dropped onto the ledge of the tunnel before him an instant later.

But, to his surprise, Simon found that the man he had just caught was not a man at all. It was a young woman of no more than fourteen years. Her short, purple hair dampened by the sweat of her brow. He had been chasing a child.

"Go."

The girl blinked her eyes in confusion. Was he really telling her to leave?

"Only seconds remain," Simon spoke hastily. "If you wish to escape, run, now!"

The violet-haired girl quickly pulled herself up and ran across the bridge, into a thicket of trees. In a moment, she was out of sight.

A gust of wind rustled by Simon's face as Valan blasted out of the tunnel and landed next to him with an angry growl.

"Where is he?" he shouted. "Did you see him?"

"No," Simon answered. "Whoever it was, they escaped. We've lost them."

Valan turned toward his old teacher in frustration. They had worked mutually for so long, faced dangers together in service of the kingdom. Never had the noble Simon Donnigan given him any reason to question their bond. At least not until that moment.

"The hour grows late," Simon said. "I think you should return to the station and report our findings. Perhaps the others had better success. I will continue alone."

"As you wish…"

~ * ~

"May I ask you something?" Morgan began, stepping up toward the altar where Foster stood with the Text in his hand. "Do you believe in all that the Text says?"

"Of course I do," Foster stated. "Although what I teach is not exactly what I study privately."

"What do you mean?"

"Well… A long time ago, the Angelic Texts were made up of fourteen Books. But some believed that the last few Books were fakes—written by charlatans who sought to change the true meaning of the Master's words. It is why most of Moralvia only acknowledges the first twelve Books, and completely ignores the final two."

"But why would you teach only part of the message, if you believe there is more to it?"

"Unfortunately, there is no other choice for a Preacher in this kingdom. To even speak of the contents of the final Books is considered heresy. Your father does not like the idea of dissenting voices."

Morgan's eyes turned away, reacting to King Brennan being referred to as his father. The idea felt so foreign to him now. Though he was uncertain about a great many things Foster thought of him.

"And Books Thirteen and Fourteen," Morgan continued. "Those are the ones that speak of the Alorium?"

"They tell of your role in the days to come. When the sky is filled with Alorium—the Angels that will bring the Master back to the World."

"But…perhaps I am not Alorium. Could it be that my…mother simply bore a child that was different? And that the Books are wrong?"

Cherry watched quietly from behind a long table in the corner, lighting a prayer lantern for her parents. Even from across the room, she could feel the tension Morgan's question had generated between him and the Preacher. It was clear that Foster was saddened by the young man's words.

"I-I apologize," Morgan said.

"No need," Foster replied. "You are still very young. Perhaps, one day, you will learn to trust in the words bound within these pages as I do. But until then…"

Foster gestured for Morgan to follow him into the next room. He sent a look back for Cherry to catch up with them.

~ * ~

"Thank you for your patronage," Aganon said as he accepted the gold from his last customer of the day.

The blacksmith's shop was closing early to celebrate Creation Day, despite his disinterest in the holiday.

As he gathered up the day's meager earnings, and put away the remaining items from the forge, he wondered what his oldest friend, Simon was up to that afternoon.

After all that had happened recently, many things in the lives of his friends were uncertain. And, though he did not agree that Prince Morgan was the savior Simon so desperately hoped to find (or that such a man existed at all), he trusted that his friend could do great things for their cause.

"If only you would give up on those foolish superstitions," he thought aloud, closing up the shop.

~ * ~

Morgan felt a great sense of calm as he shook the hand of the woman that stood before him in the prayer chamber. Never before had he seen the circular room, filled with murals that represented great events written about so long ago in the Angelic Text.

The woman was Laurien Collins, Foster's most trusted apprentice, who hoped one day to take her place beside him and lead the Southern Sanctuary. A long strip of hay-colored hair hung over her left eye as she smiled kindly at the boy. The one she hoped would bring peace to a land in need. Morgan could feel her emotion more strongly than any others. Her mind was more open somehow.

"Laurien has a very special gift," Foster continued. "One that I hope will help you to understand just what it is you mean to those of us who serve Unity and its cause."

With that, Foster took his leave, to the surprise of Morgan, and Cherry, who sat quietly in the corner, mystified by the vast paintings of ancient milestones.

"Tell me," Laurien asked. "Is Simon Donnigan well?"

Morgan did not know how acquainted she and Simon were, but it was clear that she held a great deal of interest in his welfare. When they were children, Simon and Laurien were neighbors, and they spent much of their time together. By some trick of chance, they both had gained their wings on the same day. They celebrated their rebirth as true Angels every year until, one day, Laurien chose to tell Simon of her true feelings for him. Simon, whose ambitions about law enforcement overtook much of his time, was unable to take her hand in marriage, and they began to grow apart. Their paths had not crossed again for nearly one year.

"He is well," Morgan answered. "As well as can be expected, at least…"

"I see… Are you ready?"

Morgan opened his mouth to ask what she meant, but before the words could escape his lips, a powerful force swept through him and he could feel a massive rush of warmth.

The room around Morgan seemed to vanish and he found himself dropping out of the clouds at imponderable velocity. Morgan let out a cry, unable to fathom what had just happened, until suddenly he felt the touch of Laurien's hand in his palm, and the two of them halted in the air.

"What—What is this?!"

Laurien did not speak with her voice. Her words came to him in his thoughts.

"This is my gift," she said.

Floating among the mountainous clouds in the sky, Morgan

felt that same sense of calm he had when he first shook Laurien's hand. He quickly realized that this was not real. They were still inside the prayer chamber at the Southern Sanctuary. But through the power of Laurien's Angelic gift, their minds had been taken elsewhere.

Morgan looked down to see that they were not in the skies above Moralvia. A near-infinite field of wild grass stretched out before him. But above the ground, there rested a tremendous mass of land, which hung in the air. And atop that mass was a fabulous city, constructed of wondrous silver stone, shimmering under the light of the sun.

Two mighty statues stood at the entrance, depicting Guardian Angels, wings stretched over the golden gates, each one holding flags that waved in the breeze. The flags were blue with a pair of twin white stars.

Morgan's eyes widened when he realized where they were. It was four-thousand years ago. The place called Artemis City. The first city in all the World.

Laurien and Morgan descended further into the city, until they reached the central square, as men and women walked along, completely unaware of them. Morgan let out a laugh of amazement. Few stories from the Angelic Text were as vivid to him as the ones about Artemis City, where the Angels lived in perfect harmony with the Master, and with each other. The sight of them filled him with content, and joy.

As Morgan turned his head, he found that he had been swept into a vortex that dropped him and Laurien into the secret chamber deep inside Artemis Palace, where the first king communed with the Master. It was there, at the center of the room, that he found three glimmering jewels. A blue glow flickered between them as they hung in the air above an ivory altar. Their shape was unmistakable.

"The Master's Tears," Morgan said, with a reverence that even startled himself.

They were a symbol of the bond that the Master shared with his creations, the Angels. Artemis City was the place from which the Angels went forth, and used their gifts to watch over the other beings. The beings that lived in a far-off land called Earth. It was through the power of the Master's Tears that the tunnel between Earth and Angelkind remained open.

Laurien watched as Morgan slowly began to reach for the Master's Tears in wonderment. Now was the time, she thought. She closed her eyes and focused her power.

Morgan gasped as his mind was whisked off in a vortex of thought. Morgan looked forward to see that they had not been transported to another place, but another time. A wave of hot air rushed through the room, and a great booming sound shook the walls.

Morgan ran over to the open window, throwing up a hand to resist the heat. Laurien stood quietly behind him, certain that what he was about to see would be astonishing.

Artemis City was in flames.

"This is the day," Laurien began. "The day when a group of Angels chose to break the hundred years of peace between all peoples of the World. The day when the First War began. The day the Master left the World, from which he never returned."

Through a screen of tears, Morgan watched as the shadows of Angels streaked across a crimson sky, brandishing terrible weapons. Great structures of silver, dulled by the effects of war, crumbled around them as they fought.

Morgan jumped at the sound of the door to the room suddenly flying off of its hinges in the wake of a cloud of smoke. The young man backed into a corner as a group of Angels with ash-covered swords stormed into the room, headed straight for the three jewels at the altar.

"No!" Morgan shouted.

But they ignored him. The leader of the men approached the altar with a sinister laugh.

"The power of the Master," he began. "Into my hands alone…"

Morgan recalled his memories of Book One of the Text. This man, who reached out and took the Master's Tears into his grasp, was Janir Iroshun. The man who sought to control the path to Earth, whose greed and ambition brought ruin to all of Angelkind. There was no greater enemy. For this was the day when the Master disappeared from the World.

As Janir took the jewels into his hands, an immeasurable power flowed through him, and a wave of light exploded from his body. Morgan closed his eyes, throwing up his arms in fear that the emanation would completely destroy him!

But suddenly, Morgan could feel Cherry's hand on his shoulder.

"Morgan, are you alright?"

Morgan opened his eyes to find that he was standing in the prayer chamber in the Sanctuary, with Cherry at his side. Morgan breathed heavily as he slowly began to remember that he had never left that room, and all that he had seen was only apart of Laurien's mind. What power she possessed, he thought.

"I saw it," Morgan said, still struggling to catch his breath. "The first city. I saw the war!"

Cherry could only watch as Morgan panted, slowly gathering thoughts over what he had seen and felt. Cherry did not know why, but she felt a sense of fear over what had just happened. Whatever vision Laurien had bestowed upon him might have swayed his opinion about the Text. But only Laurien knew what he had really been shown.

"The Tears," Morgan suddenly said. "What happened to them? I don't remember."

"You mean the Master's Tears?" Cherry interrupted. "The First War went on for months, as the Angels spread all over the World, searching for them."

"Yes," Laurien said, with an insistent tone. "It is not known what befell Janir Iroshun after Artemis was destroyed, but it is written that, shortly after he took the jewels, they were stolen from him. Each jewel taken by a different person, separating them for thousands of years."

"That is why," Morgan said. "That is why no one speaks of Earth now, except when reading from the Text. Because there is no one left alive that has seen it."

"Without the three Tears, the path to Earth is closed, and the true purpose of the Angels goes unfulfilled. Janir Iroshun prevented us from carrying out the Master's wishes. And the Master renounced us all for it."

~ * ~

Valan stepped through the doors to the police station in surprise at the number of officers inside. More than half their district's men were there.

Standing at the front of the room, about to address the others was Royal Guardian Sirio Nichols. He held a parchment in his hands, which depicted a drawing of a man. Valan knew the face immediately. It was Simon.

"We have received word from Rising Mountain," Sirio began. "Prince Morgan has been kidnapped, and is believed to have been killed."

Gasps rang out across the room. Valan could not believe what he was hearing. Nor could he ignore the fear in his heart as Sirio continued.

"With the help of investigators, we now suspect that the officer, Simon Donnigan, is likely responsible for the crime."

The crowd flew into an outrage. Many in that room had known Simon Donnigan for years, serving the king's law at his side. Valan curled his hand into a fist. His fears had been realized. His course was clear.

"The traitor will be found and, if possible, brought before the king to face charges. However, considering he is a suspected member of Unity, the use of lethal force has been authorized... Go with the Master."

~ * ~

Cherry watched as Morgan waved goodbye to Laurien and Foster. The experience he had, seemed to have changed him in some way. Perhaps Cherry's senses were improving, now that she was approaching the time for her wings to appear. Morgan's essence had grown different to her, in the course of a single afternoon.

Cherry and Morgan took the hands of the Ackson Brothers and were lifted into the air.

Morgan smiled as they flew. Working with Laurien was fascinating. To read about the events of the Angelic Text were such a bore, but to experience them as though he had been there was extraordinary. He hoped that he would visit them again soon. And that no one would suspect that he might be interested in learning more for the wrong reasons.

But far behind them, Simon Donnigan had just emerged from a layer of cloud, heading for the Southern Sanctuary, in the hopes that he might still arrive in time to greet Morgan as he left.

Simon had begun to descend when he suddenly felt a strange

energy. He knew who it was before he turned around to face him in the air. His red wings broadening behind him, a vengeful look in his eyes. It was Valan Wilstaff.

"Valan," Simon said, hesitantly. "What are you doing here? Did you speak to anyone at the station?"

"Enough of this act," Valan shouted. "I know who you really are."

"Of course you do. I am Simon. The same one you have always known."

"Not the man I have known. Not the man who taught me the value of the law. What you are is a traitor. And I will see you die for your betrayal."

Simon could feel a great swell of power coursing through his old comrade's arm, and knew there was nothing more he could say. Valan had activated his Angelic gift, conjuring a ball of red flame into his hand. The light of the fire crackling between his fingers reflected in his hate-soaked eyes.

Simon did not wish to quarrel with his subordinate.

Without warning, Simon's body darted off to the side in a blur, but Valan followed.

Wind ripped between Simon's golden feathers as he rushed through the air, flying low, into the city streets, in between buildings and alleyways, struggling to keep his pursuer from catching up. But he could feel Valan's persistence as he continued after him, the flame in his grasp only intensifying as they flew.

Simon summoned a sword into his hand and with the twirl of his wrist, sent the blade hissing through a wooden flagpole as he flew by. The pole began to fall just as Valan approached it, but he quickly dove deeper into the street, passing beneath the pole before it could strike the ground.

Hoping to find that his pursuer had been lost, Simon glanced back as he flew. But in the corner of his eye, he could see a great mass of flame had been hurled from Valan's hand, sent ripping across the sky toward him.

With all his might, Simon threw himself to his side, but it was not enough. He shouted out in pain as the blast sheered past his arm, scorching bits of his hair as it flew by. The blast struck the side of a large building and burst into an explosion of flame and stone that knocked Simon out of the air.

Simon's screams echoed through the land as he felt his body crash against a bed of grass and snow, at last rolling to a stop with a loud thud.

Through his dirtied fingers, Simon could feel the chill of water from the river he had just landed halfway inside, and the red mess from an open wound on his head flowed into it.

Simon felt the vibration of his attacker's feet dropping into the snow behind him. And, as he pulled himself up onto his knees to face him, Valan held forth an ivory tablet. It was the seal of law enforcement.

"By order of the king," Valan spoke. "I judge you guilty of all charges, and exercise my will to execute you now."

No hope remained for Simon to defeat this foe in a physical match. He closed his eyes and concentrated his power into his two fingers. As Valan conjured another mass of fire into his grip, Simon raised his hand and the river began to stir beneath them.

Valan looked down just in time to witness the river come alive and erupt from under him. Sent shrieking into the air, Valan's wings darted out of his back, but before he could retaliate, he found that a great serpent of water had been forged by his enemy, and Simon hurled it toward him.

Simon channeled his strength into the swirling throng as it crashed into Valan, blasting him back into a tree. Wooden branches scratched at the man's body as he dropped to the ground.

But Simon could feel his injuries sapping his energy. Soon, he would have no power left to wield, and he knew that his old student would not be defeated so easily.

Before Simon knew what was happening, a storm of flame had swept across the battlefield, from the smoldering hands of Valan Wilstaff, as he forced himself back to his feet, ignoring his fatigue. With all his strength, Simon ripped forth every particle of water below him and folded a shield of ice around his body.

Terrible thunderclaps rang out as streams of fire struck the ice one after another. Simon wiped the sweat from his brow as he struggled to maintain the barrier, and the heat behind it grew more intense. The shield began to fragment, and the cracks began to melt. Simon's power began to diminish.

At last, Simon could do more, and closed his eyes as a ball of flame broke through the shield. Shards of ice littered the grass as Simon dropped to the ground, barely coherent. His strength was gone.

Valan crushed a rock of ice under his boot as he stepped over Simon's body with a sword...

"Valan!"

The voice came from behind. Valan barely had time to turn his head before he saw the fist rush into his face, launching him across the grass, knocking him into a terrible slumber.

Before Simon drifted into a dream, he could see Aganon's calloused hands reaching down to pick him up.

~ * ~

How long Simon coasted between dream and reality, he could not know. But when he opened his eyes to the sound of whispering voices, he could see three figures through a screen of blurred vision.

Simon's body laid flat on a wooden table, staring up at a stained glass ceiling. He turned his head to see that Valan was on a second table, just next to him. And standing above him, their pearly wings drawn, were Aganon and Laurien.

Weary from injury, Simon could barely keep conscious long enough to see Aganon and Laurien, each raising a hand over the body of Valan as a warm glow flowed into him. But a weakened Simon was unable to remain awake any longer.

Day passed into night.

A great gust of air flushed through Simon's lungs as he awakened under the power of Aganon's healing. Laurien stepped out from the shadows with a smile, overjoyed to see that he was well again. Simon searched for his glasses, but found that they had been lost.

"You're alright now," she said. "It has been some time, Simon."

But Simon would not exchange pleasantries that night. He looked over to the table next to his and found that there was no one there.

"Valan was here," he said. "What happened?"

"Do not worry," Aganon replied. "It has all been taken care of."

Simon eyes narrowed. He looked at the two standing before him and could hardly believe what he was suspecting them of having done. He stepped off of the wooden table and backed away.

"Aganon," Simon said, fearfully. "You did not..."

"I healed him," Aganon claimed.

"And I changed him," Laurien said.

"What do you mean?"

"I...have a unique gift, Simon. I was not going to allow you to be taken away because of what you did for Morgan. I saw no other way. I entered his mind and implanted a false memory. As far as that man is concerned, *he* was the one that kidnapped Morgan from the castle that night—*he* is the leader of Unity, and *he* personally had Morgan destroyed."

Simon took another step back, as Laurien tried to inch closer.

"This cannot be," he said.

He looked into the eyes of the two people before him, both of whom he had known for so long. Suddenly, they were strangers to him. Strangers who had conspired to have a man killed. And all because of him.

"It is not what any of us wanted," Aganon said. "But there was no way out. Laurien implanted within him the desire to confess to the king what he...what he thinks he has done... He should be arriving at Rising Mountain any moment now."

"No."

A startling wind shot through the room, as Simon launched off of the ground, his wings exploding from his back in a rage. In an instant, he had flown through the door and was out of the Sanctuary, climbing higher and higher into the night air.

~ * ~

"You what?" King Brennan shouted in confusion.

A roar of gasps and discussion erupted across the entire throne room, upon hearing the words.

Valan stood at the center of the room, two guards behind him, staring up at the king in his chair with Sirio Nichols by his side, wearing a face of astonishment.

"I did it," Valan said. "I kidnapped Prince Morgan, and had him executed."

"But why?" Sirio asked. "This makes no sense."

Valan paused. Brennan watched curiously as a single tear rolled down the man's cheek. Whatever it was that had brought him there that night, it must have overtaken him with guilt.

"Because I…am the leader of Unity."

Brennan slammed a fist against the arm of his chair, silencing the gossip of his servants. He looked down at the young man in uncertainty. Brennan was sure that Morgan's captor was Simon Donnigan. But perhaps the reason Randir spoke his name was not to identify him as the true villain. Valan was Simon's subordinate, though Randir had never known Valan's name. Perhaps he spoke of Simon in order to suggest a connection.

Yes, he thought, *that must be it. The real traitor was Valan all along.*

But Sirio was not so easily convinced.

"Tell me then, *Unity Commander*. Where is your nest? Where are the others in your gang?"

Valan's hands began to tremble. Sirio watched in confusion as sweat began to fall across his brow. As he looked into the man's eyes, he could feel a great sense of anguish. But was it because of the terrible crimes he had committed, or was there something more?

"Look out!"

Valan raised his hand and a streak of fire blasted forth. Sirio quickly jumped in front of the throne and curled his fingers into a fist. Activating his Angelic gift, he thrust his fist forward, creating a great whirlpool of air, which rushed across the room and collided with the fire. In a flash, the flames had been extinguished.

With the swing of Sirio's arm, a current of air slashed through the floor and into Valan's body with immeasurable pressure. Sirio turned and bowed before his king as Valan's punctured body dropped to the floor and scattered into a cloud of Angelic ash.

Morgan's killer had been destroyed. Or so they thought…

~ * ~

Simon rushed through the chilling clouds as quickly as his wings could take him, until at last Rising Mountain was within his view above him. But before he could reach it, an arm wrapped around his body and twisted him around in the air.

"Simon, stop!" Aganon shouted.

"No!" he screamed. "I cannot let this happen! Valan is an innocent!"

"How can you say that? He serves the king! He would have killed you, had I not stopped him!"

"Do you not understand? We can accomplish nothing with this deception."

"I am sorry, Simon. But we do not have the luxury of waiting for a better time, which may never come. We had to act. And with Laurien's gift on our side, we may finally have a way to change this kingdom for the better."

"You have no understanding at all… We cannot change our society by forcing our will upon others. How would the Master judge us if we simply altered everyone's thoughts so that they matched our own? It is not our place to do that. And it never was."

Struck by his old friend's words, Aganon did not have the

strength to hold Simon back any further. He watched silently as Simon turned and flew back toward Rising Mountain, hoping against hope that he was not too late to make a difference. A terrible feeling of sickness quickly overtook him.

~ * ~

Morgan turned from his bed to find that Simon had finally returned, climbing down from the secret entrance to the cave below his house. He walked over to greet him, noticeably more cheerfully than he had ever been since his first night there.

"Hello, Simon," he said kindly.

But Simon's "hello" was not nearly as kind, as he simply walked right past him with a blank look across his face. Morgan tried not to notice.

"So," he continued. "When can I go back to the Southern Sanctuary? I think there is much I can learn from Laurien. Perhaps we could go tomorrow?"

Simon stopped. He turned back only halfway.

"Laurien is no longer with the Southern Sanctuary."

A look of confusion fell over Morgan's face.

"I spoke with Reverend Drake. He and Laurien had…a disagreement. Foster decided to remove her from his apprenticeship. She will no longer be a practicing member of his Sanctuary."

"But why?"

“I grow hungry,” Simon said, walking away from the former prince.

Morgan watched in bewilderment as Simon stepped over to a table with a pot of stew. He quickly gathered some stew into a bowl, but when Aganon approached from the side, Simon stepped right past him without even a glance.

Aganon’s head sulked quietly as he gathered a bowl for himself and sat alone.

STEP 5
FIFTEEN YEARS AGO

The sound of the newborn child's cries rang out across the hall as he was placed into the arms of King Brennan. The king looked down at the boy and his kind gaze immediately silenced the baby. He knew it immediately. The Master had brought them together. A son had been delivered unto him.

"I am sorry, my king," the woman who delivered the child said quietly. "The mother…"

Out of the corner of his eye, he could see the blurred image of the servant that had given all that she had in order to bring her baby into the world. Without a father, or anyone to take up the child and raise, she had nothing left, but to hope that the Master would guide him through his life, and raise him the way he should be. Her last breath was taken so that he would have many more.

"She wanted him to be named Morgan," the woman said.

Brennan looked down at the lifeless mother covered in sweat-soaked sheets, broken, spent. And then he looked back at the child.

"Morgan *Craft*," the king said at last.

The woman held in a gasp when she heard his words. "Craft" was the king's family name.

With that, King Brennan turned and walked out of the room, leaving the woman and her deceased patient in silence.

But that silence was suddenly broken when she heard a cry. Startled, the woman whipped her head around in fear. The cry had not come from her patient. She heard it in her mind. And somehow, she knew.

The woman dashed across the room and threw away the sheets that covered her patient. She had to act quickly. Her patient had been carrying more than one life inside her. And, if she did not hurry, the child that remained within her womb would die along with her...

STEP 6
ASHES

Cherry stood quietly over the counter in Simon's kitchen, chopping away at the apples she planned to include in her dish. She hoped to surprise Morgan with a meal. One that she and her mother often prepared together.

Cherry gathered the chunks of apple and dropped them into a pot.

"And now, the water," she said to herself, trying to remember all the necessary steps.

She reached down toward the glass of water on the other side of the table, but was astonished when she found that the glass had begun sliding across the counter, right into her hand.

Cherry looked curiously at the glass between her fingers and suddenly a smile began to appear on her face. She had summoned the glass with her own will.

There was no mistaking it now. Cherry was approaching the

time of wings. Very soon, she would become a true Angel, and sprout wings of her own.

Cherry poured the water into her pot with glee.

~ * ~

Galvin peered over the edge of the building rooftop and was astonished to see the number of Angels gathered in the city square. A radiant sun glowed majestically upon a sea of men and women dressed in white silk. From all across Moralvia, they had come for the service in honor of Prince Morgan's memory.

Next to Galvin sat Hadar, his legs swinging irreverently off the edge of the roof. Hadar laughed quietly to himself at the foolishness of this gathering. They were holding a funeral for a boy that was still very much alive.

The crowd stirred as fingers pointed up to the sky in anticipation for the arrival of the Royal Guardians. And out of a golden patch of clouds, they appeared. Four Royal Guardians, with Sirio Nichols leading the caravan, each one holding a section of the silver chariot between them.

In the center of the mob sat a great platform, and a large object covered with a black tarp which stood towering over the streets, taller than many buildings. The Royal Guardians landed atop the platform, gently setting down the chariot.

Sirio pulled a shimmering horn from his side and began to blow, sending a powerful sound pouring through the streets. It was the horn of the Craft Family. The very hint of its commanding sound shot a wave of citizens to their knees in respect.

Three men stepped forth from the chariot, each with the Angelic Text in hand. They were Clerics of the Sanctuary. Immediately, they summoned their wings and the pages of the books flipped open to the funeral passage. In unison, they began to recite the sacred words in their ancient tongue. As their words drifted out among the crowd, wings began to flow from the backs of the citizens, in respect for the lost prince. Wings of all colors.

At the front of the crowd knelt Mr. English, his grey wings outstretched, humbly awaiting His Majesty's appearance.

At last, the king revealed himself. Through a white silk curtain, King Brennan emerged from the chariot and looked out at the boundless number that knelt before him.

Sirio watched quietly at Brennan's side, surprised to find that the king wore a sad look across his face. Though it was not for the public's ears, it was well-known among Brennan's inner circle that he had sought to execute Morgan. So why then would Brennan weep for the loss of a boy he had already renounced long ago? Perhaps, he thought, it was simply an act, to conceal his original intent for the former prince.

The Clerics completed their recital and closed their books.

With a gesture, Brennan raised the crowd from the ground, and called the attention of every eye that surrounded him. When he spoke, there was no one among them that did not hear his commanding voice.

"Prince Morgan was one of the greatest youths this kingdom

has ever known. He devoted his life to the study of the Angelic Text, and diligent service of the Master."

Mr. English rolled his eyes as the king continued.

"His life was cut short by members of Unity. Those who would seek to spread their hate and denouncement for the Master to the noble citizens of this kingdom. But if Morgan were here today, I know exactly what he would say to that. He would assure me that this could never occur. Because the people of Moralvia are possessed of purpose. And are unified in the Master's name. And they would never stray from his teachings, or the edicts set in place by their king. All who wish to be lifted up in His glory will hold to their convictions, no matter what evil would have them stray from their chosen path."

Hadar stifled a laugh under his breath as he listened to the utter lies King Brennan spewed onto his people. This was a comedy. A charade. And he saw no reason to remain there any longer.

But before Hadar could rise from his seat on the roof, he felt a hint of power reverberate from below. He looked down to witness King Brennan call forth a pair of black wings, and a bolt of energy struck the object behind him, releasing the tarp that covered it.

Eyes widened across the crowd as the tarp dropped from around the object, revealing a great bronze statue. It was sculpted in the image of King Demitri, grandfather of Brennan. A racket sounded among the people as they realized what they were looking at.

It was the Craftian Statue, which once stood at the front of

Rising Mountain, greeting all who visited it. But 70 years ago, the statue had been destroyed by Danver Algus, who claimed that it was the end of a dark era for the kingdom. An era where those unfortunate enough to have brown wings were considered merely one-third of an Angel, forced into servitude for many generations.

Brennan looked up at the newly-rebuilt statue and saw only the great authority and majesty of it. The monument stood as a testament to the thriving of his family, and the determination of his kingdom to push through all adversity.

Many in the crowd cheered at the sight of the beautiful statue, shining brightly under the light of the sun. But many others wore uncertain looks.

Above the crowd, Hadar jumped to his feet in anger.

"How dare he," Hadar shouted.

Galvin placed a hand on Hadar's shoulder, but his brother quickly pushed it away. He sought no comfort from his anger on that day. Nor could any comfort possibly come to him when he saw the statue erected once more in the middle of the city. Galvin too felt restless, but refused to allow his emotions to rule his actions. He hoped that his brother would do the same.

But it was not to be.

Without warning, Hadar stepped right off of the edge of the roof, dropping out of the air with a furious yell. Galvin shot a hand down to grab him, but was too late. The impulsive man was out of his reach.

Wind rippled through Hadar's hair as he fell alongside the

stone building, toward the crowd below, and many Angels turned up to see him. Only moments before he struck the ground, a pair of brown wings launched from his back. Hadar defiantly yelled as his body swept over the heads of the people of the city, demanding their attention.

Brennan looked out with an icy gaze toward the insolent man that flew around the edges of the crowd. With a single nod to his men, the four Royal Guardians leapt off of the platform and rushed across the sky toward the flying civilian.

Hadar did not see the men as they flew as four blurs, shooting over the frightened citizens, headed straight for him. But suddenly, he felt Galvin's hands lock themselves onto his shoulders and angrily yank him backwards.

Hadar turned to see his hooded brother, and could feel a strong surge of power crackle between his fingers, which held tightly to his body. In that moment, he could feel Galvin's essence, and the great disappointment that filled his heart.

Hadar pulled a hood over his eyes as he turned back to see the image of the king's guards drift further and further from his sight…

~ * ~

"What is it?" Morgan asked, curiously, as he stepped into Simon's kitchen.

"Something my mother and I used to make," Cherry replied.

"I never got to give you a Creation Day present. I thought this was the least I could do."

Simon sat quietly at his desk, a stick of paperleaf in his mouth, amused at the two of them getting along. Perhaps, for one day, he would have the peace he so longed for, before the next leg of their journey began…

But just before Cherry was about to raise the lid on the smoking pot before her, the front door swung open, Galvin and Hadar quickly rushing into the house, slamming the door behind them.

Simon leapt to his feet. The Ackson Brothers were drenched in sweat, and he could feel the distress in their hearts.

"What has happened?" he asked.

"It is him," Hadar said, angrily. "That fool of a king. The Craftian Statue has been rebuilt, and erected in the center of the city, for all to see."

Morgan watched in confusion as Simon shut his eyes. He did not understand what about a statue could be such a miserable thing.

"And now," Hadar continued, "Every time we fly by the city square, we must look over and see the symbol of our oppressors staring back at us. It is offensive to all that we are. All that we have become… It should be destroyed."

"Hadar," Galvin warned.

"That will accomplish nothing," Simon said at last. "I do not agree with what Brennan has done, but we must not allow our beliefs to drive us to violence when it can be avoided."

"Damn your beliefs!" Hadar shouted.

Silence fell upon the room. The wood beneath Hadar's feet began to creak as he took a step back, slightly surprised at his own words.

"I...I am sorry. But I do not see how more protests and demonstrations are going to change the fact that, whenever I enter the Moralvian Square, I have to see the face of the man that expected me to be a servant, and to sit at the back of the Sanctuary, away from the other visitors, because my wings were brown."

Cherry turned her head to find that Morgan was no longer facing the others. His head sunk low as his back was turned to the rest of the room. How terrible it must be for him, she thought, to hear such dreadful things about the family he was raised with.

The shouting of the three men grew louder, but became as distant echoes to Morgan and Cherry, who stood separately, unmoving, in the kitchen.

At long last, like darts through a still cloud, Morgan's voice broke the clamoring.

"I must go."

Simon, Galvin, and Hadar all turned at once toward the young man, his face still sunk low from behind.

"Morgan?" Simon asked.

"The Master's Tears are scattered about the country," Morgan said. "Brennan believes that, with their power, he will hold the key to bringing back the Master. This is why I must go. To find the other Tears."

"The *other* Tears?" Galvin asked, probingly. "Does that mean you know where one of them is already?"

Morgan turned his head to face the eyes of those that stared at him intently. It was something in which he found great difficulty. To speak openly, to so many, about such unsettling things. He did not even know why he kept it from them.

"One of the Master's Tears," he said, "is already in King Brennan's hands."

Morgan pushed past the looks of surprise across the faces that gawked back at him, as he continued to speak.

"If these jewels do bestow as much power unto their wielders as the Angelic Text says, then Brennan cannot be allowed to possess any more of them. He has sent many warriors in search of them already. They cannot be allowed to succeed before we do."

Simon watched in astonishment as young Morgan Craft spoke. He had not imagined that the boy he smuggled out of the castle would ever speak as he was now. He was too overcome by his own troubles to have seen how quickly the boy had begun to grow. Though perhaps he did not realize the magnitude of his words.

"Artemis City is the birthplace of Angelkind. Where Angels walked side-by-side with the Master. And where the Master's Tears were held for hundreds of years. Or so the Text tells us...I must go there... If there is no other way to stop what my...what the king has done, then I must."

"It is too dangerous for you to go yourself," Simon spoke.

"The city is cursed. Forbidden. If we go at all, it will be without you. And you will—"

"No!"

Galvin and Hadar turned to Simon as he had just been silenced by the youth.

"No more waiting. No more requests… I am Morgan Craft, Prince of Moralvia, heir to the king's throne."

A great power swept across the room as Morgan's blue-feathered wings rushed out of his back and spread around him like a great banner.

"If these wings on my back make me Alorium, then so be it. I will fly. And I will not stop until I reach the shores of Artemis City and find the Master's Tears…"

Cherry's heart beat rapidly in her chest. Never had she felt such intense energy flowing from the boy that stood before her. His intentions were clear. And there was nothing any of them could do to stop him.

To the surprise of the others, Simon slowly descended to one knee and bowed his head humbly. Morgan looked down with trembling eyes. He had not been prepared for the words he had just let out. And there was no way to take them back…

STEP 7
THE ROAD BACK

The silvery glow of the moon shimmered in Morgan's eyes as he sat on the roof of Simon's house next to Cherry. The sky had not been so clear in such a long time, as a cool breeze brushed past them under the diamond-studded stars.

Long had it been since Cherry had looked up at the stars with her father, who recited to her the most wondrous poems. They were long nights, much like that one, just before her father would set out on a journey the following morning. She thought it fitting she found herself there with Morgan, who had a journey of his own to begin.

"I do not see why I cannot come along," Cherry said.

Morgan stared up at the stars, having hoped not to argue under such a spectacular sky.

"I understand you wish to help," Morgan replied. "But there could be danger. It is said that Artemis City has been cursed. And Brennan's soldiers could be there."

"All the more reason for me to join you."

"I have wings. I can take care of myself."

"I'm still older than you. What if something happens and—"

"That is what I have Simon for. And Aganon has volunteered to join us as well… Now, please. We shouldn't argue anymore."

Cherry did not know why she chose not to speak of the changes that were happening to her. That perhaps she would be able to help, if they would only wait a bit longer, for her wings to develop. Instead, she simply pointed up and smiled.

"See that group of stars there," she said, kindly. "That is the First Angel."

Morgan looked up into the heavens and his eyes found a cluster of stars, which formed the faint image of a man with massive wings.

"What is he called?" Morgan asked, innocently.

"He has no name. He was simply called Angel. The forefather of us all."

Morgan watched the First Angel shimmer amid the darkness of the sky and a great calm fell over him. With all that was at stake for him and those around him, it was in this one moment that he could feel a sense of contentment. Cherry had rescued him from it all once again…

~ * ~

Cherry stepped into the East Border Marketplace and it came alive before her. Men and women flew above, and strolled back and forth between her as she walked through the crowd.

A leather bag across her shoulder, she squeezed between two very large men in an effort to reach the stand which held many freshly picked fruits and vegetables.

Before she could reach the stand, the sight of a tower came into sight, from the corner of her eye. She turned up to see that it was the Craftian Statue, protruding up from the mass of people in the square. It cast an enormous shadow over the crowd. Even after three days, the whispers of discontent could still be heard over its creation. The city police were even stationed to protect the monument, though Cherry did not understand why. She did her best to ignore the unpleasant thoughts.

Cherry breathed deeply of the beautiful foods as she walked around the stand, looking for apples.

The crowd had grown so thick after only just a few minutes that she found herself pushing her way around the stand, while the man behind the counter scurried about to help his customers as quickly as he could. All Cherry wanted was a few apples.

But suddenly, Cherry turned her head up to find that an apple had just popped out of its place on the stand and rolled over to her. The apple landed into the palm of her hand before she even realized how it had happened.

Her powers had reacted again. It took only a stray thought to set them loose, reaching out to grab the apple and bring it forth. Cherry suddenly felt a great feeling of warmth on her back. They were coming…

"Did you do that?"

Cherry turned around nervously, surprised to find that

Laurien Collins stood before her. That same lock of blonde hair hung over her eye. She greeted the young woman with a pleasant smile.

"Laurien," Cherry said. "It is nice to see you again."

"And you as well. But...something is different about you."

Cherry did not know what to say. No one else around her—none of those she thought were closest to her—had noticed a change in her. And yet this woman, which she did not know well at all, immediately felt it. That which lingered beneath the surface.

Laurien looked down at her and her blue eye twinkled under a ray of sunlight. A flash of intuition came.

"You are approaching the time of wings," she said.

"Yes," Cherry answered, flattered that she would notice. "I did not think anyone knew."

"Simon must be helping you with your new power. I can already sense a great deal from you."

"Oh no. Simon is not even here. He and Morgan set out—"

Cherry threw a hand over her mouth when she realized that the man across the counter was standing there, waiting for her to purchase the apple she still held in her hand.

"Oh, my. I completely forgot."

Cherry dug a hand into her bag to find the money, but before she could pull them out, Laurien had already handed coins of her own to the merchant.

"Perhaps this is not the best place to talk," Laurien said.

"Perhaps you are right," Cherry agreed, feeling foolish.

"Then let us go."

With that, before Cherry could react, Laurien had taken her hand and the two of them lifted straight up into the air and out of the marketplace. Cherry could not help but let out a laugh, as she was carried along by Laurien in one hand, and gripped her apple in another. Morgan and Simon had gone, but perhaps she had found a new friend in this beautiful Preacher's Apprentice.

Laurien smirked as she flew with the crimson-haired girl at her side. Cherry had presented an opportunity. To repair the chasm between Simon and herself. For him to at last acknowledge her for the woman she knew she was.

~ * ~

Kraven let out a sinister laugh as he stretched out an arm to reach down and choke the life out of his former colleague.

"Merry Creation Day," he whispered.

"STOP!"

Simon's eyes widened. Could that voice really have belonged to whom it sounded like?

Kraven recalled his arm in irritation, looking up into the sky, from which the voice had come. And up, through the sheets of snow falling from the heavens, he could see the faint image of a young man, standing at the roof of the Tower of Life. A flicker of power emanated from his blue wings as they extended around him. It was Morgan Craft.

"How sweet," Kraven laughed at Simon, still writhing at his feet. "You brought me a gift as well."

"No, wait!" Simon yelled.

It was too late. Kraven leapt up into the air and took flight, shooting up toward the blue-haired boy with beastly delight.

But, before Kraven had time to reach the top of the tower, Morgan dove straight down toward him. Kraven cried out in astonishment as he felt Morgan's foot drill into his face, sending him rocketing out of the sky, slamming through the roof of the old library, crushing a table beneath him before hitting the floor.

His body racked with injury, Kraven looked up through a cloud of debris at the sight of a man backing away into the shadows. It was the librarian, Leeland Rote.

In a terrible fright, he turned to run from the man that had just dropped through his roof. Kraven began to rise just before the entrance to the library, making it impossible for Leeland to escape through the front. He wiped the sweat from his brow as he ran toward the second exit on the opposite end of the library.

But just as his hand touched the cold doorknob, he could feel a great swell of power, and the entrance suddenly was ripped open by the force of another Angel exploding through the front door.

Leeland frantically opened the back door and ran out as quickly as he could, but a splinter of Angelic power slashed across the back wall, as the terrible sounds of battle echoed forth from within the shaking library.

The librarian turned just as he summoned his wings, but before he took flight, he was astonished to see who it was that had just entered his library. The sight of his blue wings was extraordinary. His blue hair flew, kicked up by an unnatural wind as he wielded an impossible power against his shape-shifting enemy.

"Prince Morgan?"

~ * ~

Leeland stood in amazement at the cold, marble floors he stood upon, as a magnificent beam of sunlight poured into the king's throne room through the window to his side. It was at the highest point in the entire castle. Never had he entered the great halls of the royal family. His only wish would have been for it to be under more pleasant circumstances.

Sirio Nichols stood flabbergasted at King Brennan's side as they listened to the man's story. A suspicious glare sent Leeland's gaze elsewhere. Leeland had not considered until that very moment that they may think him a liar, and hold him for questioning. Or worse…

But Leeland considered it his duty to come forward and tell all that he knew. He had left the city to visit his sick mother in a neighboring land shortly after the loss of his library, and had only heard of the tragedy of Morgan's death upon his return. It was then that he realized that the young prince may not have been killed after all.

"I do not know if it will help at all," Leeland continued. "But I thought you should know. I did not quite believe it myself.

Prince Morgan, with wings. It almost makes you question the teachings of—"

"Mister Rote," Sirio interrupted. "We need you to understand that what you saw is not for the ears of those around you. What you have just told us must never be spoken of outside the walls of this chamber."

"S-Sir?" Leeland asked, in confusion. "If the prince is still alive. If the prince has wings, when he is clearly too young for that, then the people—"

King Brennan rose from his seat on the throne and a dark power rushed across the room. Leeland struggled to keep from shivering under the immense weight of that terrible energy he suddenly felt from the man that stood before him.

"Leeland Rote," Brennan spoke. "Were there any others you saw that night? Perhaps Valan Wilstaff, one of the local officers."

Leeland swallowed against the lump in his throat as he pulled forth the memory of that night once more.

"Local officers… Yes. Yes, there was another there. But it was not Valan Wilstaff. It was the blonde man. I believe they call him Simon… That is all I know. I swear it."

Leeland watched curiously as Sirio and the king exchanged looks of confusion and surprise.

After all that time, Brennan thought. Could it have really been Simon all along? Could they have destroyed an innocent man? But that was impossible. Valan Wilstaff had confessed to the kidnapping, and attacked him in that very room. A terrible thought began to creep into Brennan's mind. What if there were more like them among his officers?

"Mister Rote," Sirio said, breaking the silence. "My words still stand… You will not speak of that night to anyone for as long as you live. To do so would be a treasonous act, punishable by execution, and a blatant offense to the Master Himself."

Struck by fear and isolation, Leeland fell to his knees at their mercy. He no longer cared about how or why they would conceal the truth about the prince. All he wanted was to go home…

~ * ~

"Do you miss him?"

Laurien paused as she entered the room with a small tray with two glasses of tea. She had not expected the young woman who sat below her to come forth with such a question so abruptly.

"You mean Simon," Laurien said, taking a seat on the floor next to Cherry. "Yes, I do miss him. I regret that we were unable to work through our friendship many years ago. But I believe that we will be together again. He will see the error in his actions."

Cherry shirked her confusion over that last statement, as she accepted the tea from her new friend.

"I see that you have someone you miss as well," Laurien said.

Cherry quickly drank of her tea to avoid responding. Laurien had reached out with her mind and brought out the thought. The thought of Morgan, off on some quest that she was not apart of, and could perhaps take him from her indefinitely.

"I believe he must feel the same way," Laurien continued.

Before Cherry could respond, Laurien had already extended her hands at her sides. Out of her back, a pair of white wings stretched. Cherry set her glass of tea down and hesitantly lifted her hands.

"So, are you going to use your gi—"

But the moment Cherry's hands made contact with Laurien's, an incredible rush of energy flushed through her, and she gasped. Laurien had activated her Angelic gift, and entered her mind.

Cherry closed her eyes as she could feel Laurien's essence intermingled with her own. Memories that were once so vague suddenly came rushing into the light, more vividly than the years beyond them would allow. And Laurien experienced them all, as though they were her own.

Laurien's fingers shook as they tangled between Cherry's. Never before had she connected with the mind of someone quite like this girl. The pain of days long passed was extraordinary. Never would she have thought that such a kind young woman be harboring such desperate rage beneath her enchanting eyes.

A single tear fell from Cherry's closed eye as she realized that Laurien had witnessed her past. The time of her childhood. When her parents were taken and executed by the king's soldiers, under his order. But there was more.

Laurien had never felt such resistance in all her life. Somehow, Cherry was able to suppress her thoughts. Perhaps, she thought, she should stop herself. But when a stray image of Simon flashed between their thoughts, Laurien ignored her hesitation, and pressed harder.

The child.

Laurien gasped. The morning before Cherry lost her mother—the final morning they spent together—she had told Cherry that she was going to have a baby brother or sister. And then her mother died.

A great surge swept through Laurien when she realized she had awakened some dark corner of Cherry's thoughts, that the girl had locked up tightly, hoping never to let it escape.

The force was overwhelming. Laurien's heartbeat quickened as she struggled to keep from being swallowed up by the bottomless negative energy she had uncovered, in her search for memories she had no business finding. She cursed herself for what she had done. She was there to help Cherry discover her Angelic gifts, but had touched something much more.

Cherry's eyes shot open, and the first thing they saw was the blurred sight of Laurien, whose body had been launched across the room by an eruption of power—a power that had come from within Cherry herself.

Laurien's wings stopped her just barely before colliding with the back wall. She looked down at the young woman with wide eyes, astonished at what she had seen and felt. She threw her hands behind her back to keep Cherry from noticing that they were still trembling, a residue of her power still coursing through her fingers.

"I'm sorry," Cherry said with tearful eyes. "Did-Did I do that?"

Only then did Cherry realize, as she rose to her feet, that she felt something behind her. She turned her head, and one of her wings reached around to greet her eyes. Red feathers. Her wings had finally appeared.

Laurien stepped forward, hoping that the girl would not sense the nervousness in her heart. In all her years, Laurien had never felt such devastating anger in the minds of those her gift had touched. Nor had she felt such a rapid growth of power spring forth from a child first gaining wings.

But Cherry did not know this. And Laurien decided that there was no reason to tell her. It mattered only that she had done as she hoped, and that Simon would be pleased. He would see that she was worthy of his affection once more…

~ * ~

Cherry walked along the street at night with Laurien at her side, unable to keep from smiling. At long last, she had become a true Angel. She looked forward to the time when she could tell Simon and Morgan what had happened, with Laurien's help.

She had only wished that she was able to fly right away. But that was for another day. And then, when the time was right, she would discover her Angelic gift—the power that was unique to herself. As the two of them strolled down toward Simon's house, she could not help but wonder what it might be.

But suddenly, Cherry's look of joy fell away when a crackle of firelight caught her eye. Cherry held her breath at the sight of Simon's house, flames hissing wildly across the roof, smoke flowing out of every window and chimney.

The voice of Sirio Nichols echoed through the night air as he shouted orders for his soldiers to search the house. It had not been long before they discovered the secret underground chamber, and several Unity members hiding within.

At last, through a thick cloud of smoke, the sword of Hadar Ackson emerged, slashing its way into the crowd of Royal Guardians. With a ferocious battlecry, Hadar whirled his blade through the air, striking down as many soldiers as he could, in a desperate attempt to stop the attack on the house he was charged with protecting.

An axe flew toward the back of his head, but was blocked by the sword of Galvin, whose mighty fist sent the attacker spinning to the ground.

Back to back, the Ackson Brothers stood, their weapons swinging wildly about. The two warriors lifted into the air as the soldiers surrounded them, rushing in from all angles. But before they could give battle to anymore, a great wave of air blasted through the crowd, sending the brothers crashing back to the ground, weapons flung from their hands.

Sirio lowered to the ground, a concentration of air swirling between his fingers.

"Enough," he shouted. "I will defeat these fools myself."

Galvin struggled to shake away his disorientation, but the rush of air that struck them down had penetrated his very skin and ripped his clothing. His enemy was too strong for even the both of them united.

Hadar pulled himself to his feet to fight on, but Galvin gripped his arm in an effort to grab him out of harm's way.

Sirio smirked at the thought of them believing they could escape him, as he channeled his Angelic gift, summoning a great wind into the battlefield. He curled his fingers into a fist at his side, a concentration of air collecting into it.

With that, he thrust his fist forward, and an immense explosion of air rocketed across the battlefield toward the brothers. There was no time to dodge such an attack. Without thinking, Galvin threw himself in front of Hadar, who cried out in horror.

Hadar looked up with terrified eyes, waiting to see his brother fly apart before him. But it did not happen.

A terrible sound rang out as the ground seemed to erupt behind Galvin, and the earth shook. Howls of astonishment filled the air.

Galvin turned around to find that Cherry was standing just behind him. Hadar moved over to find that Cherry was completely undamaged, and a pair of crimson wings stretched out of her back, from which a great power flowed.

Laurien watched from the shadows, dumfounded at what she had seen. Through some unimaginable power, Cherry had found the strength to fly, and the very appearance of her wings caused Sirio's attack to be deflected back on itself.

"Leave…them…alone…"

The voice that echoed eerily from Cherry's lips was not the voice they knew. It forced its way out from some dark gulf within her. One that she had kept buried deep inside. Until now.

Galvin raised a hand to place on her shoulder, but quickly yanked his arm away an instant later. Her body was like a vessel of fire. To touch her was to touch flame. And in his moment of contact, he could feel a terrible anger from her essence. It was as though the Cherry he knew had been absorbed. Swallowed up by the rage beneath.

"Destroy her," Sirio shouted.

With that, twenty Royal Guardians darted through the air, weapons drawn.

Laurien suddenly dropped to her knees at the sight of them, unable to explain a sudden, unexpected spell of weakness that came over her. But then she realized it.

The Royal Guardians flew toward the girl with furious intent, but in the eyes of their minds, they saw a great wall of fire suddenly leap out of the ground. Sirio watched in confusion as the soldiers all spun out of the air, turning back with cries of terror. He could not know what his men saw and felt. It was an illusion.

"Impossible," Laurien let out, as she struggled to breathe. It was Cherry's Angelic gift. She had drained Laurien of her own essence, and used her gift to attack the soldiers. Laurien's power was now Cherry's power. Whether she willed it to be or not. And when Cherry wielded the power, it was intensified ten fold.

Sirio called forth a whirlpool of wind around his fist, ready to strike the young Angel down. But just before he could thrust it forward, it was ripped right out of his grasp and dispersed in the air.

Sirio tried to gasp in surprise, but there was no air for his mouth to draw from. The blood in his veins grew cold as he could feel his own essence slipping away. He looked over to the young woman, whose red eyes grew darker and darker, until there was nothing left but a terrible abyss of hatred.

Silence struck the battlefield…

Galvin and Hadar both looked to each other in fear as they realized what was coming. Before they could escape, the power shot out of Cherry in all directions. The force of a hurricane rippled through the air in an ever-expanding whirlwind.

Galvin, Hadar, Laurien, Sirio, and every soldier was thrown about the street like cloth dolls by a wind of incredible strength. Every sight, sound, and sensation was drowned out by the maddening racket of debris being cloven from the ground and out of surrounding houses, spinning into the air.

Laurien did not know how long it had taken for her body to drop out of the sky, crashing halfway over the side of an old balcony, but it took even longer for her to awaken from the pains of her fall.

One eye opened to the sight of a red blur streaking across the heavens. The other eye opened before a devastated street, covered in great boulders that had been forced from the ground, among the bricks and wood of half-destroyed houses.

Reaching out from under a wooden board was Galvin's hand, as he slowly drifted out of a dream.

Whatever Cherry had hoped to do, it was more powerful than she could control. She had not simply attacked the soldiers, but the entire battlefield itself. And the power she unleashed did not care who was a friend and who was an enemy.

"What have you done?!"

Galvin quickly pulled himself up to find that Hadar had landed on the balcony of a nearby house, angrily shouting at Laurien. Galvin leapt into the air and flew over to find out what was happening.

"I-I did nothing," Laurien said, nervously.

"You lie," Hadar shouted back. "Did you not think that Simon would tell us? About what you did with the police officer. We know your ways, Laurien Collins."

"Hadar," Galvin spoke, hoping to temper the situation. But his brother refused to listen.

"You worked your powers on Cherry," Hadar continued. "Forced her to attack, not caring who she harmed in the process."

"That is not true," Laurien said through a cracked voice. "I…I knew there was a change in her, but I did not think her capable of this. I did not send her here to fight."

"But you did do *something*," Galvin said, suspiciously.

"She wanted help. She wanted to learn about her gifts. I entered her mind, but what I found there… I did not know that one girl could have that much anger bottled up inside. It is possible that seeking those memories is what changed her. The power she possessed was too strong for her to control, and it used the pain of her memories to force its way out. The power is in control now. Not her."

"We must find her," Galvin said. "Stop her before she harms herself. Or someone else."

"You will fail," Laurien insisted. "I felt her essence, more strongly than any of you could. It is pure rage that fuels her. And it will only grow stronger. You will not survive."

"Thank you, Laurien," Hadar said, sarcastically, "for proving to us just how far you are willing to go to manipulate those witless enough to be around you."

Galvin tried to stop his brother, but he continued.

"You are a fool. And a coward. And as much as you may convince yourself of otherwise, there is no place for you in the world that Simon is trying to create. You are a waste on this world."

Struck silent by his words, Laurien lowered her head as Hadar turned his back on her without regret. She was no longer worth his time. He would be content to simply ignore that she ever existed.

"It is time to go," Hadar said to his brother.

But just as the two of them had called forth their wings, a frightening power fell over them, and they both dropped to the ground, forced into a deep slumber.

Laurien stared down at them angrily. Her gift had at last returned to her. And if Hadar thought her a monster for using it against them, then she was willing to accept that.

There was no turning back from the road she walked on now. Laurien stepped off of the balcony and dropped into the night.

~ * ~

A matchstick struck the ground and ignited into a tiny flame, glowing amid the darkness of night. The officer brought the match to his face, lighting the stick of paperleaf in his mouth.

He and his four comrades stood watch over the Craftian Statue, as they had for the past several nights. None of the men were particularly happy with their new appointments as guardians of the monument. The very idea seemed positively foolish. But this was what their king had called upon them to do.

"Let me have one of those, friend," said one officer, gesturing to the paperleaf stick.

"Perhaps one day," he replied, "you will find some of your own."

He kindly tossed a stick of paperleaf over to his partner and began to pull out a match for him to light it.

"No need," he said, and he activated his gift, generating a tiny flame on the edge of his finger, which he used to light the paperleaf.

His friend smiled.

But their smiles quickly faded when they all began to sense a strange presence. All eyes turned to the blackened skies above the city square, where a tiny spot of red began to emerge from the veil of darkness.

It was not long before they realized that it was an Angel, headed directly for the monument, long after the king's curfew. One officer hurriedly pulled forth his ivory seal.

"By order of the king, I command you. Halt!"

"You command?" said a shrill voice from the sky. "You command nothing!"

Screaming out of the shadows, the red-winged Angel flew straight into the man, ripping him off of the ground in an instant. The man's tablet shattered as it hit the ground, and his body was slammed against the base of the statue with such strength that he fell limp at her feet.

The man's three comrades all conjured swords, which trembled in their hands, as they struggled not to show fear from the monstrous essence that flooded over the streets from the fiery-haired girl. Her eyes burning with a furious, red power, she turned to face the three men, and the sight of them only increased her anger.

Those fools—agents of the king—who thought they could control her. Thought they could stop her from destroying the monument and taking the vengeance she knew she deserved.

Spitting out his paperleaf, an officer called upon his gift, fashioning a snake of fire into his hand. It came shrieking forth from his grasp a moment later, ready to strike down the young woman once and for all.

But the fire did not touch her. The three officers watched wide-eyed as Cherry raised her hand, and the flames were absorbed into it as though they were apart of her. The man that had attacked her suddenly dropped to one knee, as he could feel her steal away his essence, piece by piece.

A ball of spectral flame came hissing forth from her palm a moment later, spinning above her hand. The three guards quickly abandoned their station and disappeared into the night sky in fear.

Cherry spun back toward the statue that towered over her, casting a seemingly endless shadow behind her from the moons above. She looked up at the face of the statue and the ball of fire in her hand began to pulsate with vengeful power as her anger perpetuated.

The time had come. Nothing else existed but her rage, and the desire to release it upon any and all who would stand before her. There was nothing left for her but destruction.

Cherry thrust her hand forward, blasting the fire from her grip, and it shot into the base of the statue. In a flash of Angelic energy, an explosion tore its way through the statue's legs, sending a wave of flame and stone into the air, as the remainder of the monument slowly began to fall forward.

Cherry did not move. She simply watched, her eyes a bottomless void, as the emotionless face of the statue drew closer and closer to her own, and its shadow fell deeper behind her.

But just before the statue could touch her face, a great force swooped in beneath it, and snatched her across the street in an instant. A monstrous roar erupted from the ground as the statue came crashing into it, scattering into countless fragments of rock and ash, which spilled about the street in a parade of destruction.

Stones fell around Cherry's face as she was forced to the

ground by the arm of another Angel. She could feel her essence, and knew who it was that had tackled her before she saw her face.

Laurien cried out as she hit the ground with Cherry, but before she could offer any words for the young woman, she felt a pair of red wings strike her body, tossing her back into the air.

Cherry twirled back up to her feet, the power of her wings surging through her just as strongly as ever, as Laurien struggled to land on the pile of debris that was the Craftian Statue.

"You dare to challenge me?" Cherry spoke, through a voice that Laurien did not recognize.

"You are not yourself," Laurien said, her wings draped over her like a cloak. "I come to help you find it again."

Cherry let out a laugh that ripped the air around her.

"What a fallacy," she said. "You, who sought to bring this power out of me, now come to see it put back? You are a fool!"

"Yes," Laurien said. "I am."

Cherry's eyes widened when she suddenly realized that Laurien had activated her Angelic gift, and a dagger of thought was hurled into her mind without warning.

Cherry struggled to resist, but Laurien fought her with a determination that she had never known. Like a hammer through a wall of stone, Laurien's powers slammed into her thoughts, breaking down the layers that kept her true self from emerging.

Startled and angry, Cherry conjured a fireball and threw it at her enemy. But Laurien's unwavering focus sapped her concentration, and the flame did not strike her as it was meant to.

Laurien gasped in horror as she could feel the sting of the fire as it shot past her arm, bursting into a blaze when it landed in the ground behind her. But she did not move. She was unable to. The power she fought was as such that, if her thoughts strayed from her task for even a moment, she feared her mind would be completely destroyed.

Suddenly, Laurien could feel a piece of her essence slipping away, and she knew what was happening. But Laurien did not waver. Her wings shot open around her and a powerful glow emanated from them. Cherry let out a shriek of anger as she realized Laurien was preventing her from stealing her essence. But the cost of such exertion was slowly killing her.

"Why do you do this?!" Cherry shouted, though not with her lips. *"You cared nothing for me! I felt it. Your only hope was to use me to catch the attention of another. Why then do you not just leave me?!"*

"It is because of that," Laurien that, *"that I stay!"*

Cherry's legs wobbled as she struggled to find the concentration to walk forward, slowly marching toward her enemy with hate in her eyes. Hate over what she had done to her. Hate over what she had been made to do. Hate over what the world had taken from her. And hate over what she had done in return. She had to get close enough. Close enough that she would need no concentration to end this. She would do so with her bare hands.

Laurien kept to her conviction, as she drew closer and closer to the true Cherry, buried somewhere beneath that avalanche of anger and power. She ignored the pain shooting through her veins. She pushed the churning of her stomach deep inside. Blood flowed from her nose. Every inch of her trembled uncontrollably. But she could not stop. Only seconds remained before her work was finished.

Cherry stared into Laurien's eyes as their faces drew closer. Cherry's hands lifted up at her side and rocks began to drift up weightlessly into the air, the power of the two Angels reaching their apex. Her fingers were around Laurien's throat moments later.

With a single twist of the wrist, Cherry could destroy her enemy. But just before her hands could move, a great chill swept through her, and Laurien's body fell lifelessly at her feet.

"Laurien!"

Cherry dropped to her knees in a panic, tears streaming from her face as her wings vanished behind her. The last thing Laurien could see before she was overcome by darkness was the color of Cherry's eyes. They were just as they were when she had first met her.

Laurien smiled contently as she slowly drifted into the night air as a wisp of Angelic ash.

STEP 8
SEVEN YEARS AGO

Kiran Ellison froze in place as the old sack he had been carrying fell out of his hands, spilling oranges out onto the cobble-stoned street before him. A chilling wind brushed through the blue hair of the eight-year-old boy as he glanced around at the men and women that stood in the marketplace with hateful looks in their eyes.

The people of Jeruma City never looked so terrible to him than at that moment. Kiran had spent his entire life there, but had never known any cause to dislike this place in which he lived, where his adoptive parents raised him. Until now.

Kiran kept waiting for his mother and father to rise up from the ground, wipe away the blood flowing from their kind faces, and tell him that it was all right. But it was not. Surrounded by the stones that had been hurled at his parents, Kiran watched in horror as the two people that meant the most to him in the world slowly turned to ash and blew away like leaves in the wind.

It was their wings. Kiran's father often warned him not to stray too far from him when they were out in the city, for there were some who did not like the color of their wings. Kiran thought that perhaps he was too young to understand, but he could not see why his parents having brown wings made them unclean in the eyes of their neighbors.

"He tried to grab me," said a voice from across the street. It came from a shopkeeper, telling her story to the two police officers at the scene. "He wanted to hurt me," the old woman said. The look on her face did not express fear, as Kiran would have expected.

The very idea was preposterous. Kiran's father was the most gentle, kind soul he had known. The only reason he would have had to reach out to her at all would be to pay her for the doll he wanted to buy for his son. Doubtlessly, the old woman had screamed, in irrational fear, and incited a mob. The result of which was the end of Mister and Misses Ellison, right there in the streets of Jeruma City, that place where Kiran was raised. That place he would grow to hate…

Kiran looked up with tears in his eyes at the two officers that began to walk over toward him. They did not look as he thought an officer should. Their faces were not kind, or concerned. In Kiran's eyes, they were glad to be rid of those brown-winged scum, and irritated that they now had to deal with their child. Perhaps, Kiran thought, they might even be hoping he would resist them, so that they would feel justified in using force against him. But Kiran had all the justification he needed.

The two officers suddenly stopped in the street when they realized that the rocks that had been used to stone the Ellisons to death had begun rising from the ground, floating buoyantly around them. A crackle of energy fell over the streets, as the townspeople began to feel sick. The officers looked down in astonishment as a pair of blue wings extended from the child's back!

The officers summoned swords into their hands, but a crushing force caused their fingers to collapse in on themselves, and their weapons dropped to the ground.

With unbridled fury in his eyes, Kiran Ellison rose from the street and hurled himself through the air toward the two men, dumfounded with fear and confusion. Their cries echoed across the entire marketplace as a flash of light blinded all who witnessed it…

STEP 9
DEAD CITY

The overpowering light of the sun poured through a patch of great clouds, filling the morning sky with a majestic glow. A warm breeze rustled through Morgan's hair as he flew with the others further and further away from Moralvia, until at last, they could no longer see it at all, consumed by the towering, grass-covered mountains of the south.

Morning passed into afternoon, and Morgan's wings grew tired. He looked around him and found nothing but two unhappy faces on either side of him. Faces that belonged to Simon and his longtime friend, Aganon.

Simon let out a sigh of annoyance as he glanced over to Aganon, flying alongside them. It was not his choice to bring him along on this journey. Aganon had volunteered on his own, upon hearing of it from the Ackson Brothers.

Aganon flew with a determination in his eyes. Simon's anger did not escape him. In fact, it was this, more than anything else, that brought him there that day. Too long had he and Simon lived and fought together to build a greater kingdom for their people. The best road back to their friendship, he felt, was to assist him on this quest. Even if he did not believe in it.

Morgan knew nothing of where they were headed, or what they might do when they arrived. He hesitated to ask. The look Simon wore across his face was not one that would have welcomed questions. And Morgan was not certain that he was ready to ask them himself. This was, after all, Morgan's plan.

They must have passed the borders of King Brennan's domain by now. At long last, through a blanket of clouds, they had arrived. The place that Brennan's forces would not dare cross into. For it was a forbidden place. It was Artemis City.

Morgan's eyes widened as they drew nearer to the great city, which rested on a tremendous mass of earth that floated in the air. Amid the rolling curtains of grey cloud, Artemis City shimmered under the streaks of daylight that passed through it.

Morgan remembered reading wondrous poems about the rise and fall of the great Artemis City as a child, wishing that his father might one day take him there to see it himself. But that would never happen, for reasons that Morgan preferred not to think about.

And as Morgan grew closer to the great entrance to the city, he began to realize that the finery and splendor he had dreamed about had long since faded from the place.

The once magnificent Guardian Angel statues that stood outside the gates were now half crumbled and stained by the fires of war. The spears from which the city's flags were hung, once held proudly by the Guardians, had fallen long ago.

Morgan looked up in sadness at the old, broken capital that stood mangled in the distance. No longer did the silvery city glow with majesty. Whatever remained among the toppled structures and hollowed monuments was a remnant of the most horrific war.

At last, Morgan dropped from the air, landing atop the head of the westernmost Guardian Angel, its face now scarred and covered by ever-growing moss. He stared out at the unfortunate site of the once proud city of legend, as Simon and Aganon landed just behind him.

"Long have I desired to see this place for myself," Simon said, quietly, as he looked out in wonder at the site, filled with such history. "The Angelic Text tells us that this was the first city of our world. The place where Angels and the Master lived together in harmony. But a group of defiant Angels led an attack upon the city, seeking to control it for themselves. When the last sword had been swung, and the last arrow was shot, the few who remained alive found that the Master had disappeared, and a curse had fallen over the city. And so they left, never to return."

"A curse," Morgan said, still staring into the distance.

"If you believe in such things," Aganon said, his arms crossed.

It was not unusual for Simon to hear such words from his friend, Aganon, but on this day, with all that had happened between them, they held more weight than before. Simon could not hold his tongue.

"And what does that mean?" Simon asked in annoyance.

And Aganon could not help but perpetuate it.

"It means that no one has been here to challenge the old belief for many hundreds of years," he said. "I do not fear what I do not understand. Nor do I live my life according to what others have told me."

"And you think that is what I do? And that I am a fool for it."

"Those are your words."

"Yes, and so are these… I will not toss away my soul in an attempt to control others simply because I disagree with their ways. I am better than that."

"How dare you!"

But suddenly, Simon felt a rush of energy from behind, and turned to find that Morgan had jumped from the Guardian Angel and begun soaring low into the city without warning.

Aganon stopped and looked out in confusion, as the blue-winged boy slowly drifted out of sight.

"Morgan?" Simon shouted, as he lifted off of the statue to find him.

A sigh escaped Aganon's breath as he watched his old friend rush down into the city to follow the boy. With an uncertain frown, he jumped into the air.

~ * ~

Morgan's wings shivered in the wind as he whipped them along through the air, flying intently through the destroyed city, slowly flying faster and faster. And he did not know why. But there was something beyond his field of vision that he knew he had to find. Something so distant and faint that he somehow feared that he would lose whatever it was that called to him if he did not hurry. Simon and Aganon were of no use to him. Long gone by the time he had reached the palace.

Morgan looked up in awe as he slowed his approach to the grand structure before him. Even in its decayed state, the palace was a powerful sight. A testament to the diligent brilliance of its ancient architects.

But the sudden presence he had felt was too strong to ignore. Morgan quickly shrugged off his fascination with the palace and rushed inside. Through a charred open window he flew, rushing down the cracked ivory halls, where tapestries and paintings hung by threads on the walls, if they were still hanging at all.

He knew this place.

Somehow, though he had never truly been there before, he felt as though he knew precisely where to fly. And as he continued deeper into the structure, the presence grew more powerful.

Finally, he came upon a doorway at the end of a long corridor. The doors to which had been knocked off of their hinges, pieces of which were scattered about the floor. But beyond the door, Morgan saw nothing but darkness. An unnatural darkness, which filled the room into which the doorway lead.

Morgan's feet touched the cold marble of the floor as he put away his wings. He slowly inched closer to the arch of the door, trying to peer inside, but saw only faint impressions of the room inside.

A ghastly stench crept out of the room, as Morgan suddenly became hesitant to step inside. Yet he knew that this was where he must go. That great presence that pulled him forward had brought him here. To this terrible place in the center of the palace.

Morgan inched his way further into the chamber, covering his nose from the rotten smell. His body began to tremble as the air grew colder the further he stepped in, though he saw no open windows, nor felt any breeze.

Through darkened vision, Morgan's eyes desperately scanned the shadowy room, hoping to find it. That thing that had brought him there. It was then that he realized that he had seen this place before.

As he stepped up to a small ivory altar, in what must have been the center of the room, he knew that it must be. The place he had seen in Laurien's vision. The secret chamber that held the Master's Tears.

Morgan's shaky hand began to reach down toward the altar to touch it.

But before his fingers hit the table, a sudden noise behind him rang out, and his head fearfully spun around.

Morgan backed away from the sound, as the echo of a falling object vibrated across the room and down the endless hall. He squinted his eyes, desperately hoping to see what it was that could have caused something to fall.

At last, the image of a tall shadow, slowly swaying in the

darkness, came into view. It skulked its way through the room. Soon, it stood in front of the door, the only source of light from the windows outside shining in from behind it.

It was only then that he began to sense the essence of an Angel. Like water through a collapsing damn, the dark presence flooded the room. A ferocious anger permeated the frozen air as the figure stepped forward. Morgan felt as though he would suffocate from the strain as that dark, chilling presence grew stronger, and it continued to advance.

Morgan found himself slowly backing away, as the sound of the figure's footsteps grew louder and louder. He could not help but let out a gasp as he felt his back push itself into a wall. There was no space left for him to back into.

"Hello, Morgan," the figure spoke. "I have waited so long to meet you."

Morgan's eyes widened in surprise. He knew his name.

Morgan watched in confusion as the Angel stepped closer. The look of his face horrified him. A pair of hollow eyes as black as night stared back at him through a veil of tattered, dark hair. The skin about his face looked as though it had been torn, though there was no sign of blood. As though his face had been drained of it long ago. Beneath the man's cloak was an old suit of red and gold armor, rusted and broken.

The sight of him made Morgan wish to look away. But before he could, his gaze fell down toward the strange jewel that hung from his neck, resting over his breastplate. The moment his eyes found it, he could see a faint hint of blue light flicker from within the jewel. There was no mistaking it. This creature that had called to him from the shadows was wearing one of the three Master's Tears.

"Who… Who are you?" Morgan asked through a haze of cold breath.

"Royal Guardian Kaster Nichols."

Morgan stood in bewilderment at his answer. Long had he known the Royal Guardian known as Sirio Nichols, who served at Rising Mountain for many years under the king. Whispers of the story of Sirio's father could be heard all through the castle. Stories which told of a great friendship between Kaster and Brennan. But why then was he there, in that accursed city, after years of absence from the king's side?

"Long ago," Kaster said, "King Brennan sent forth a brigade of soldiers in search of the ancient talismans called the Master's Tears. It is said that when the three tears are brought together, great power will be afforded the one who holds them. Power enough to open the gateway to Earth. Or perhaps bring the Master back to the World. I was among those sent out to find the two Tears that remained lost. And I alone returned with one."

Morgan again was confused. He had always known that his father held one of the jewels since long before his was born. But he did not know that a second had ever found its way into Moralvia. And as Kaster continued, Morgan began to wonder if this man knew anything of his son while he was away.

"Always had I been a loyal servant of the rightful king of Moralvia. It was only after I had tasted the sweet flavor of true power that I began to question His Majesty. As a Royal Guardian, my duty was to present the king with the Master's Tear. But I could not. For, in my presence, the power of the jewel showed me things that I could not have otherwise seen.

In visions beyond my imagination, the future stretched out before me, and it was a cloaked in darkness. Whether through their intentions, or through sheer accident, people such as King Brennan had ruined the kingdom I had fought so long and hard to protect. I could not hand over the power with which I knew he would do this to my home.

And so, I hid the jewel. When the king came for me, he begged me not to keep this secret from him, but I refused. I told him what I had seen, and what I knew he, and others like him, would do if he continued down the path he had chosen for himself. But my words fell upon deaf ears."

Morgan listened as the man slowly paced the floors of the room, telling his story. But the man's voice grew more angry as he continued.

"My oldest friend looked upon me with eyes that I had never seen before. In moments, the whole of our history had been lost in a chasm of bitterness! And that was when he took it."

"Took what?" Morgan asked, nervously.

Kaster looked down at the young man with those cold, lifeless eyes, and a single wing ejected from his back. Morgan watched in fear as the man slowly turned around to reveal one faded white wing, feathers ruffled with decay. And, in the place of a second wing, there was only a small, malformed stump, which protruded unnaturally down his back, covered in old, twisted flesh.

Morgan struggled to hold his tears as he realized what had happened. Only in the dark stories that his father forbade him to read had he heard of Angels whose wings had been cut away. Wings were the last connection to the Master. The essence and power of the Angel were set to reside there. To remove such things were a punishment worse than execution. For in death, there was absolution. But the life of an Angel whose wings were cut was one of unending darkness and despair.

"I waited," Kaster said, in a hollow, shrill voice. "I waited here. For the time that I knew would come, when the world could be changed. So that my fate would not befall any others. That my fate would bare some sense of meaning. I have prolonged this wretched life as long as possible. I had to. Because I knew you would come."

Morgan could deny his tears no longer, as they trickled down his face. Kaster waited. Through a life of shadow and pain, Kaster endured, with only the faint hope of meeting him. A terrible feeling fell over the former prince. All the horror of Kaster's existence. It was all for *him*?

"I…I'm sorry," Morgan let out.

"So am I," Kaster replied.

"You?… For what?"

"For this!"

Suddenly, Kaster turned and leapt into the air, rushing across the room toward the blue-haired young man. Morgan let out a cry as a skeletal hand reach out to grab him. He quickly threw himself to his side in fear.

The marble of the floor cracked under the heavy boots of the former soldier as he landed, turning his head with a monstrous howl, like that of some horrible beast. With the flick of his wrist, Kaster sent the ivory altar flying into the air, rushing over toward Morgan.

"Stop!" Morgan shouted, wings extending from his back.

A great power exploded from Morgan's wings, shattering the altar an instant before it could touch him. He rose from the floor in a mix of fear and despair, shards of ivory scattering at his feet.

"Do not do this!" Morgan pleaded, as he threw up an arm to block Kaster's fist. He could not do what he knew Kaster was asking of him. After all that had been done—all that this man had been forced to endure because of his family—how could he even think of killing him?

"Of all people," Kaster shouted, hurling his fists at Morgan with such speed that they became as a blur in the darkness, "I know that there are things that must be done. Every day that passed since the choices your father and I made, counted toward this end."

Morgan let out a cry as a gust of wind broke through his arms along with Kaster's powerful fist, sending him shooting across the room, crashing into the wall near the doorway.

"Stop!" Morgan pleaded. But there was no reasoning with him. The creature that lifted into the air, one wing stretched at his side, was waiting for an end. And, one way or another, he would have it.

A flicker of light struck the jagged edge of a dagger, conjured into Kaster's scraggly hand.

Overcome with fear and sorrow, Morgan could feel the pulse of Angelic lightning surge between his fingers. Morgan looked up with trembling eyes as the sound of Kaster's words.

"Farewell, Alorium."

With that, Kaster hurled himself down toward the frightened boy, his dagger raised to slash him. But the dagger slipped out of Kaster's hand as he was struck by a brilliant streak of blue lightning, which tossed him backwards through the air. Morgan shut his eyes as the Angel slammed into the back wall and burst into ashes.

When Morgan's eyes were opened again, they immediately were drawn to the object on the floor, glistening in the last remaining light from outside. Wiping tears from his face, he rose from the floor and walked closer to the twinkling object.

There, sitting amid the ashes that vaporized all around it, sat the Master's Tear, unsoiled by the death of its last holder. The sight of it was just as radiant as it must have been hundreds of years ago.

Shirking the uneasiness of what he had just been forced to do, Morgan reached down to grab it.

But the moment his finger made contact with the jewel, an incredible force exploded forth from within it. Morgan felt a surge of energy flow through him as the room was bathed in light.

And as the unbridled power of the amulet consumed him, he could hear them. The voices of all those that had ever touched the jewels. And all those that ever would. Their essence—their very lives—were apart of his. And he was apart of theirs.

~ * ~

"Wait!"

It was the third time that Simon had heard Aganon's voice shouting at him from afar. And it was the third time that he ignored it, as he continued to search for Morgan.

He did his best to follow the trail of his essence. But something in that place prevented it. As though a wall had been lifted between them.

Simon breathed a sigh. Perhaps there were walls between all of them on that day. It seemed to him that the paths of all three of them had begun to diverge. And part of that could have been because of him. But how could he forgive what Aganon had done, after all that had happened?

As the last light of day began to fade, Simon came across what must have once been a garden. He dropped down into the cobble-stoned lane near the place where Simon guessed the flowers would be arranged. But in their place were weeds, rooted deeply into a rotting patch of earth. To his right there sat a lake, which had become a murky, green swamp, stretching out across the entire valley, separating the two halves of the city.

When Simon looked out across the lake, his eyes found that a large building had toppled over, now half consumed in the swampy waters. At the top of the debris, there sat a large spear, stabbed into a block of stone. Simon quickly realized that this was the site of a famous battle. The last, and most hideous battle Artemis City had ever known. The Battle of Sharivan Lake.

Simon's wings shivered as a great feeling of uncertainty swept over him. Something was happening. Something emerging from the lake…

Aganon landed just behind his old friend with an irritated grumble.

"You could not have waited for me?" Aganon asked.

"You were not that far behind," Simon answered. He refused to turn around to face him.

"Perhaps not. But I called out to you. Did you not hear me?"

"Why are you here, Aganon?"

"How can you even ask that? I do now what I have always done, when you needed it. You are the one who has changed. Not I."

"You fool…"

Aganon's eyes narrowed at Simon's words. But before Aganon could respond, he was halted by a strange feeling. He sensed the essence of another…

Suddenly, the swamp began to stir, and a figure in rusted silver armor rose up out of the sludge with a beastly shriek. Its red eyes glowed menacingly at the sight of the two Angels.

Aganon gasped.

"A spirit!" he shouted. "Look out!"

Aganon ran up to pull his friend out of the way, but the spirit jumped forward and thrust its hand right through Simon's chest as though it were made of thin air. Simon cried out as the power of the spirit coursed through him, suppressing his essence. Soon, he found himself unable to move, or even breathe if the spirit did not allow him to. Simon could not even scream as the creature's face came closer to his own, and a foul smell came rushing out of its mouth, forcing its way into his lungs. The calloused face of the creature pushed itself into Simon's.

In an instant, the spirit had completely buried itself within Simon's body. And when Aganon reached out and grabbed him by the shoulder, Simon's body whipped around and shot a fist into his chest.

Aganon fell back into the ground, gripping his chest in pain and confusion.

"Simon?" he asked.

But Simon was gone. He could sense only one being standing before him, and it was not his friend.

Simon's eyes became a bloody red as the monster inside him curiously looked down at his hands with a devilish thrill.

"What are you?" Aganon shouted, rising to his feet.

The voice that answered did not belong to the Simon he remembered. It was cold and lifeless. As though the night itself had begun to speak.

"Look upon me and feel the true magnitude of your failure. Your action. Your inaction. Your arrogance. Your petty conspiracy. Tremble before the weight of your own evils… I am your end."

The creature with Simon's face raised a hand, and a great

explosion of swamp water erupted from the lake behind him. Into the air, a massive serpent of green mire rose. And at the twist of Simon's wrist, it was sent blasting its way down toward Aganon below at immense pressure.

Aganon curled his hand into a fist and stomped across the field with all his strength, quickly tackling Simon off of his feet. A column of water slammed into the ground just behind them as they flew, ripping a crater into the ground before the two men fell into the lake with a loud splash.

In the vacant blackness of swamp water, Aganon saw nothing, and felt only the fist of his old friend. Even now, as the two warriors sank deeper into the swamp, the creature continued to fight. While Aganon struggled to hold what little breath he had, the spirit had no need for air. Unable to rise to the surface, as Simon's grip pulled Aganon further down, only seconds remained for him.

Simon, Aganon thought. *You asked me why I am here. And here is my answer!*

With that, Aganon's wings flowed out into the murk of the lake and he thrust his hand onto Simon's chest. A hail of bubbles came rushing out of Simon's mouth as it released a guttural scream.

Without warning, Simon felt a warm power shoot through him from the palm of Aganon's hand. Even at the bottom of those stirring waters, he could see the white light that passed between them, coursing through his veins, burning away the essence that did not belong there. The spirit tried to pull itself from Simon's body, but the light only grew stronger, until the spirit was completely consumed.

Up above, the surface of the lake had grown deceptively still…until a large hand shot up out of the water and dug its fingers into the ground, dragging Aganon and Simon out of the lake with the last of its strength.

Simon turned onto his shoulder, coughing up water. He quickly turned back to tend to Aganon, who was lying on his back, greatly weakened by what he had done.

Simon rested a hand on his friend's chest. When Aganon's gift touched him in the water, he could feel his essence more strongly than ever before. He felt the terrible guilt and sorrow that Aganon carried with him. The fear of Simon's absence from his side.

"Are you all right, my friend?" Simon asked.

"There are many things I do not believe," Aganon spoke. He took Simon's hand into his own and clinched it tightly. "But this…I believe in this."

"As do I," Simon said.

But Aganon noticed that Simon's face suddenly changed when he looked back toward Sharivan Lake. Aganon pulled his head up to see what had caught his attention.

One after another, the spirits began to rise. Up out of the grime that became the home of their ashes, the dead Angels crept forth, their red eyes fixed upon the two friends. They were interlopers. Trespassers into this den where so many Angels had fought and perished.

This was the curse that fell over Artemis City. Those whose

lives were lost here were trapped for all time. Lying in wait to make victims of all who dared to return.

Simon struggled to pull Aganon to his feet as the spirits continued to rise, slowly walking closer, ready to destroy them both. A pair of wings made of nothing but stripped bone extended from the first spirit's back. It smiled menacingly as a sword appeared in its hand, ready to strike…

"STOP!"

The voice was like an explosion ripping across the heavens, tearing its way through the clouds, sending a chill through the bodies of all who heard it.

Simon and Aganon looked up to see where the voice must have come from.

Landing atop the broken structure that sat halfway into the lake, Morgan Craft's wings stretched out around him as he rested a hand on the ancient spear stuck into the stone.

Simon squinted to see that Morgan's eyes were closed. Even as the creatures that surrounded him slowly drew nearer to the young Angel, he did not react. Soon, every spirit that had risen from Sharivan Lake had turned toward him, ready to attack.

It was only then that Simon realized that there was a jewel hanging from Morgan's neck. And as the creature came closer to him, it reacted.

Morgan's eyes opened, and a great wave of power blasted forth from the Master's Tear, sweeping across the entire land. The instant the spirits were touched by his gaze, the entire army was thrown back in a single motion. The screeching of countless dead

Angels could be heard across the land as they were struck by a terror they had not felt in ages.

Aganon searched his thoughts for an answer but found none, as he watched in amazement. The creatures were scurrying away from the boy, frightened beyond belief, desperately dragging their way back into the swamp from wince they had come.

Simon dropped to a knee in reverence. For him there was no doubt. The spirits were ancient Angels, who had walked with the Master Himself. Who else but an Alorium, a wielder of the Master's Tear, could halt their attack?

Morgan stood upon the broken building, a remnant from that vicious war fought so long ago, and he could feel the warmth from the fires that once burned across the valley. He heard the cries of warriors rushing into battle. The power of the Master's Tear reached out across the city and the memories flooded his mind.

Morgan's hand clinched tightly to the spear at his side, and he made a silent promise that it would not happen again. He looked up into the sky and took flight. Rising Mountain awaited...

STEP 10
WALTZ

"Can't catch me!" Gwen shouted gleefully as she ran through the grassy fields of the east, as her three friends hopelessly tried to keep up with her.

Gwen was always the fastest of the four children. In any race, the others knew they would not be able to beat her. Of course, it did not stop them from trying again.

It had been the first day in their village that was not terribly cold and wet. The clouds were blanketed in the hot glow of a bright sun. The distant chirping of birds could be heard amid the children's' laughter. Finally, they were allowed to leave the village and be outside again.

But as the afternoon came to a close, and the sun began to rest upon the mountainous horizon, the children were ready to return home.

As always Gwen led the group, as they ran up the hill that lead back through the field toward their village. But as Gwen first arrived at the top of the hill, the others were surprised by her sudden stop.

Slowly Gwen's friends appeared around her as she stared out beyond the hill toward the sight of the village. And slowly they began to realize what it was they were staring at.

The village burned.

Shadows dashed across the oncoming night, cast about by wild flames, which tore their way through the houses and buildings and surrounding forest that was Gwen's home.

Up in the sky, clouds were parted by the approach of three enormous objects, pushing their way through the air above the village. They were airships. And they were headed toward Moralvia…

STEP 11
MOMENTS

"Laurien!"

Cherry dropped to her knees in a panic, tears streaming from her face as her wings vanished behind her. The last thing Laurien could see before she was overcome by darkness was the color of Cherry's eyes. They were just as they were when she had first met her.

Laurien smiled contently as she slowly drifted into the night air as a wisp of Angelic ash.

Her head sunk low, Cherry knew not how long she had sat there in the middle of the broken street, weeping. But as she raised her face from her hands, she felt a presence. As she turned up onto her feet, she could sense the police officers rushing to the scene, searching for who might have caused such appalling destruction.

Cherry stood frozen in place, as the shadows drew nearer from out of the distance. She had the power to fight, but a great sense of dread crept into her heart. She had no wish to harm anyone. And if she acted too hastily, she feared what she might do.

But suddenly, just as the faces of the men came into view, they were startled by the echo of a great thunderclap ripping out of the sky. Down from the heavens, blue lightning rained, tearing into the ground before the officers, who quickly rushed back into the darkness.

Cherry looked up to find Morgan's hand reaching down from above. In a moment, her hand was in his, and they flew off into the night.

"Quickly!" Simon shouted, as he and Aganon swept past them from over their heads.

A surge of emotion passed between Cherry and Morgan as their hands met in the air. It was clear to each of them that the other had changed since their last meeting, under the stars. For better or for worse, neither of them would ever be the same.

~ * ~

"Hold still, you old fool!" Aganon shouted, as he struggled to keep Hadar's arm close enough to his hand to heal his injury.

"Well, if you would work a bit faster…" Hadar said in jest.

Aganon sighed in annoyance as he channeled his gift, slowly repairing Hadar's arm, as he and his brother continued their conversation.

The panels on the walls of the old inn room glowed dimly, casting a soft yellow light over Galvin's face as he took a seat on the opposite bed. The placed was rather cramped, though Galvin would never remark upon such things.

Aganon sat and listened as the two of them argued over their current circumstances. To hear them speak this way was nothing new for him, though their situation had changed significantly since their quest to Artemis City.

Aganon had returned to a home to find that it had been ransacked, doubtlessly by agents of the king, who sought to put him in shackles. And it was not much different for most other members of Unity. In recent days, many trusted friends were forced to relocate, or simply vanished under dreadfully mysterious circumstances.

Hadar suddenly felt Aganon's grip grow tighter around his arm and shouted out from the sting.

"Watch that!" Hadar said.

Aganon simply frowned behind his moustache, continuing the work on his injuries. But his thoughts dwelled endlessly on their state of affairs. He did not know how much longer he could sit there, inactively.

~ * ~

Simon looked out of the window of his inn room and found that he could see his own reflection in the glass. But one of the window panes was cracked, splintering his image into twisted shapes. He looked into his own eyes, not certain what it was he searched for, but hoping desperately to find something.

It had been only days since he left Moralvia with Morgan. But in that time, he had lost his home, his career as an officer of the law, and his reputation as a man of honor and peace. And, however indirectly it might have been, Simon could not rid himself of the fear that Laurien's death was of his own making.

And then Simon turned around. There, curled up on the bed next to him, was the one thing he had left. Through fire and darkness, he marched onward so that this young blue-haired boy would survive, and fulfill what he knew was his destiny. For however much longer the Master would allow him, Simon knew that his life would be intertwined with Morgan's.

There was no turning back. And perhaps there never was.

~ * ~

As Morgan quietly placed the old ink pen to the tattered piece of paper at the desk, he suddenly realized that he had not even held a pen since the day he left Rising Mountain. In school, with Mr. English.

What an irony, he thought, that he would remember such a thing on the eve of his return to the castle; and that, in the meantime, he felt as though he had learned more than he ever could have there.

When the note was finished, he signed his name at the bottom of the page, and folded it on the table for Simon to read when he awoke that morning.

Morgan turned around to find his friend lying flat on his back on the hard wooden floor, next to his own empty bed. Simon had given so much for him. And he would continue to give for as long as he lived. Morgan silently bowed his head in gratitude, as he walked out of the room.

As Morgan stepped quietly down the dark hallways of the inn, he knew who it was that followed him, but said nothing until he reached the building's exit.

"This is where we part ways, Cherry."

"But why?" she asked, as she stepped into the light of the twin moons from outside. "Where will you go? And for what?"

"I go to Rising Mountain. To retrieve the second of the Master's Tears… If you knew what I know of the jewels' power, you would understand. It is too dangerous to leave in the hands of…him. Especially with the third jewel out there somewhere, waiting for his soldiers to find."

"I understand just fine. What I don't understand is why you are leaving your friends behind. We can help. I can help."

Cherry struggled with her thoughts as she spoke those words. After all that had happened to her, she was terrified of unleashing that dark power she knew was still apart of her. But as Morgan was about to walk out of that door, perhaps for the last time, she could think of nothing else to say to keep it from happening. She would risk it all to remain at his side.

Cherry searched Morgan's eyes for an answer—something that would make him understand what she was trying to say. Morgan looked upon her face, desperately holding back all the thoughts that might cause him to stay. But the emotion of the crimson-haired girl flooded over him. He could not resist her heart anymore than he could resist his own.

"Thank them for me," Morgan let out at last.

Cherry watched as Morgan turned with trembling eyes and jumped into the air. His blue wings shot out from his back as he rushed up through the starry sky, disappearing into the night.

"Goodbye…"

STEP 12
THE FATHER AND THE SON

"Execute Order 13!"

Brennan gasped as he darted up from the sweat-soaked pillow at his back. He grasped the rim of his blankets and threw them aside as he pulled himself up onto the edge of the bed, burying his face into a shaky hand.

Another dream had robbed him of his sleep.

In his slumber, he found himself walking through an endless valley of wild grass, on a chilling winter night. He crossed his arms nervously as the cold was unbearable. The blackest sky hung over his head, utterly emptied of stars, and a terrible wind began to race past him. Whispers sounded from the darkness, but there were no faces from which their voices could have come. And then the fire came. The wild grass began to burn, and as Brennan ran to keep away, he found that it was all around him. Brennan threw a hand into the air, hoping to fly away, but his feet never left the ground. As the fires grew more intense, Brennan turned his head around, horrified at the sight of his own wings lying in the grass, drenched in a red mess, having been slashed off of his back. Before Brennan could reach down to them, he realized that the fire had reached his face, and consumed the feathers. The last thing he saw—the last thing he would always see—was the shadows of two young children flying overhead—as he was swallowed up by flame...

As Brennan pulled himself to his feet, he could still feel the sting of the fire on his skin. As though some part of him was still there in the dream. Almost as though it were real.

Perhaps, Brennan thought, there was more to that nightmare than he had allowed himself to believe. But he did not presume to know what it was, nor what he could possibly do about it.

As Brennan conjured some clothing from the wardrobe near his bed, his thoughts dwelled on the events of days long past, though still so clear in his own mind. To learn that his adopted son might still be alive, the result of some elaborate deception by a band of deviant peasants. That all of this would happen within his own domain, without his knowledge, beyond his ability to change. The thought was maddening.

The green glow of the panels across the walls greeted him as he stepped out of his chambers and into the hall. Long had it been since he walked the corridors alone at night. Not since the early years of Morgan's life among them, when the child would often sneak down into the food stores to find some sweets that he knew he should not have.

As Brennan stepped by a pair of windows, a flash of intuition fell over him, and he turned to look.

A vast sky opened up before him as the first hint of a golden sun came creeping across the blue horizon, bringing light to the city down below. But a strange sensation pierced his thoughts as he stared off into the distance. And it was not the first time he had felt it. Before Brennan could tear himself away from the feeling, he sensed that the worst of his days were not yet behind him.

The king stepped back from the window, and walked on.

But what the king did not realize was that, at that very moment, just above the window, a young man was clinging to the wall outside the castle, feeling much as he was. Through the power of the Master's Tear hanging around his neck, under his shirt, Morgan Craft had seen his dream just as clearly as he had dreamt it himself. The chill of winter still lingered in the breeze, which flowed around him as he sat against the wall, uncertain of what to do next.

But Morgan sensed another presence, and in the corner of his eye, he could see a guard gliding over from across the front of the mountain, on patrol. Morgan launched off of the wall, rushing across the heavens in a blue blur. He latched back onto the wall on the far side, beyond the patrolman's field of vision.

Morgan let out a slight laugh at what he had just done. Unburdened by the fear of being discovered as a youth with wings, he had learned to fly faster than anyone else he had ever known. Perhaps, he thought, he was one of the most powerful Angels in the World now. All he needed was the time and will to bring that power forth.

But it was power that brought him back to Rising Mountain.

For the amulet that hung around the neck of Morgan's father was a danger too great for him to ignore. If he was to get his hands on the third jewel, which was lost for centuries, who knew what terrible depths he could end up leading the kingdom to? For a moment, Morgan regretted asking Simon and the others to let him take up this task alone.

Alas, the time to turn back had passed. And so, Morgan closed his eyes and invoked the power of the Master's Tear. And in his mind, he found his father again, tracing his presence through the castle…

~ * ~

The panels on the walls of King Brennan's bed chamber filled with light as he stepped into the room, closing the door behind him. A long day had ended in another set of disappointments, as the king's men continued to search for the remaining members of Unity.

A great bed of pillows awaited the king as his heavy coat hit the floor and he walked over toward the dresser on the left side of the room. At the desk rested a small jewel box, where Brennan would place his amulet every night before bed. At his side, there was a large, wooden wardrobe, decorated with the white crystals passed down through generations of his family.

Brennan opened the jewel box and began to grab the chain around his neck. But when he did, he again felt that strange flicker of intuition. And something more…

Morgan shouted out in shock as Brennan's hands exploded through the walls of the wardrobe and grabbed his body from inside, yanking him right through the wood and crystal, chucking him through the air. Wind whipped past him as he flew uncontrollably across the room and slammed against the far wall.

Before Morgan could hit the floor, his body stopped in the air, as he pulled himself back up, curling his hands into fists. He had been discovered. And, though startled by his father's attack, was not injured.

"You disappoint me, Morgan," King Brennan said, angrily, slowly coming to grips with the levity of the situation he had just been thrown into. "That trick did not work when you were nine years old. What made you think it would work now?"

"Spare me the fond memories, Brennan," Morgan answered, impudently. "I care little to remember the false love you fed me all those years."

Brennan reacted to being referred to by name, rather than by the title of father.

"Speak not to me about false love, when you hid in the shadows and kept secrets from me for years."

"And whose fault was it that I kept them to begin with?"

"You… You insolent little fool. If you came here to kill me, then do so now, and save me from your ignorant rantings!"

"It is not your life I came here to take!"

"Fine! Then I shall take yours!"

Brennan furiously summoned his wings, which stretched out of him like living shadows, smothering the light in the room until there was nothing left. But Brennan stepped back in astonishment when he realized that, emerging from the darkness, sheering through the waves of power that flowed from his body, Morgan Craft pushed his way toward him at impossible speed.

Before Brennan realized what was happening, he felt himself be snatched backwards. Rock and stone flew about him as his body crashed through the wall of his room and down the hall.

Across the corridor, Mr. English had just turned the corner, his eyes focused on a book in his hand. But the pages of the book suddenly began to flip themselves unnaturally, until a mighty wind tossed it out of his hand. Mr. English looked up with wide eyes, astounded at the sight of King Brennan and Morgan Craft flying down the hallway, hurling fists at each other with such force that the very walls around them rippled and shattered. In a matter of seconds, a thousand attacks had been thrown, turning the corridor into a storm of debris.

Mr. English cried out as he realized the two blurred figures were headed his way, utterly unaware of his presence, their raging battlecries ripping the fabric of the air that surrounded them. But just before they touched him, a flash of blue lightning sent them smashing down through the floor.

Brennan moved with speed beyond sight as the castle garden was torn apart by bolts of Angelic lightning, tirelessly shot forth from the hands of his blue-winged attacker. Brennan waved his arm and an entire wall erupted under his power, hurling an army of grey bricks toward Morgan as the king rushed into the next room. But a cloak of power-soaked wings protected Morgan as he threw himself back at his adoptive father with unrelenting determination.

The king gasped in shock, as he blocked a kick, deflecting a wave of power that decimated half the dining room. How, he thought, could a boy of only fifteen years be so unbelievably powerful?

All across the castle, soldiers gathered in confusion, searching for some answer to the terrible rocking that had ravaged the building, and sent the servants into a panic. Rushing through the entrance, a Royal Guardian walked in just in time to feel a pulse of energy that struck the room.

The essence felt familiar to him. For he had felt it before. Sirio Nichols had just arrived at the castle to report his investigations into Unity, only to find that one of those members had made their way into the castle.

Sirio called forth his wings and flew through the trembling corridors of the castle, rocks and dust falling all around him as he followed the trail of energy that he was sensing. The path led him to the uppermost point in the structure, where a massive window of stained glass rested.

Sirio watched in amazement at the blurred after-images that dashed across the room, blasting great craters into the walls and floor with the mere swing of their arms. Sirio gathered a concentration of air into a fist, ready to strike the moment Morgan Craft gave him an opening to attack. At last, he saw Morgan land across the window, and he thrust his fist toward him with all his might.

But to his surprise, Morgan raised a hand, and a tidal wave of Angelic power shattered the stream of air, sending a massive explosion of wind and energy in all directions. Before Sirio could think to evade it, he found himself forced back against a wall, knocked into a deep slumber.

But instead of being thrown back along with him, King Brennan flew right through the blast and his hands locked around Morgan's throat as the two of them were blasted through the window.

Unphased by the cold air under the light of the approaching sunset, the two enemies dropped out of the sky, Morgan struggling to break free of the king's grasp. Overtaken with rage, and filled with a power that had become seemingly limitless, he barely felt their bodies crash into the balcony several levels down, which nearly collapsed under the strain.

Still holding the boy down with one monstrous hand, King Brennan pooled into his fist a power like he had not brought forth since before Morgan was even born. A power that most certainly would blow right through him, and the balcony, and whatever might be below that in the process.

But the king faltered. He looked down at the sapphire eyes of the child as they stared back up at him. The grip of his hand loosened. Energy in his fist faded.

Morgan looked up at the man that was once his father with trembling eyes. What was it that made him stop? Was he unable to bring himself to do what he seemed so willing to do that night he learned his secret? Or was he experiencing the same feeling that he was…?

Without words, Morgan and Brennan both turned and stood up. Wind rustled past them as they looked out toward those dark clouds marching across the heavens in the distance. That terrible intuition that had plagued them. Each had assumed that they were merely sensing each other, and the painful thing they might have to do when they finally met once more. But that was not it.

Morgan could feel the power of the amulet vibrating next to his heart. And he knew that Brennan felt the same from his own. Morgan opened his mouth, as a precognitive voice spoke through him.

"He's coming…"

~ * ~

"I think we should go and find Morgan."

Cherry looked up from her bowl of soup and realized that everyone at the table was staring at her, blankly. Except for Hadar. He sat with a bemused smile at her innocent interruption of their silent dinner.

"I know he told us not to follow him. But…"

No one answered her. The fact that they were still alive, hiding behind the walls of an old inn, in the middle of Moralvia, was reason enough to be happy. But there was no way the few remaining members of Unity would risk leaving to find a single boy. Except for one.

Simon Donnigan blew a ring of smoke from his mouth as he stood by the window of the inn's dining hall, uncertain of what to do. He felt it was his duty to protect the boy, but now he had gone, and might never be back. Perhaps Cherry was right.

Simon rose to his feet, to the annoyance of Aganon, and many other allies they had reunited with upon their return.

But before he could speak his intentions to find Morgan, something stirred within him. He plucked the paperleaf from his mouth and turned around as a strange feeling flushed through him.

Up in the sky, he could see something emerge from the clouds. Not an Angel. But something much larger. A huge, wooden object, the shadow of which was slowly stretching across the entire city block.

Simon startled his friends by walking right outside, into the open, where anyone that knew his face could report his whereabouts to the king. But what was slowly covering the sky above was too important.

"A ship…"

~ * ~

Purple light flowed over the hooded man as he entered the main deck of the vessel, the wood in the floors creaking with every footstep. Everywhere he walked, men and women in black robes dropped to their knees at the sight of him. A smile appeared on his face, still cloaked in shadow.

"We've arrived," he said, quietly. He spoke as though he needed no one to tell him. He simply knew...

"Yes, my lord," answered one of his many servants. "The others should be just behind us."

"Then let it begin... Alorium Hai."

The entire room repeated his ancient words, in perfect unison. *"Alorium Hai!"*

~ * ~

Morgan took a deep breath as a great swell of power flowed through him. It was like those three giant vessels, floating across the heavens over the city, were reservoirs of pure Angelic energy, overflowing with the most intoxicating power that had ever touched him. He looked over to King Brennan, expecting him to know what was happening, but the man's look of confusion matched his own.

Brennan watched, struggling to keep his hands from trembling, as he could barely see the image of Angels in black robes all descending from the ships and gliding over the city in waves. And, in their hands, they held massive spears, pulsing with destructive power.

"By the Master's hand..."

The moment Brennan said the words, he knew that what he had uttered in nervousness was more accurate than he had at first realized.

A name jumped out at Morgan from the darkness in his mind,

prompted by the amulet at his neck, or perhaps by something else, out there in the sky. He had never heard the name before in his life, but it grew more familiar in his thoughts as it escaped his lips. And it filled him with dread...

"Kiran Ellison...."

STEP 13
SIEGE

Morgan's heart beat rapidly in his chest as he could feel a strong emanation from the image forming in the distance. A great cloud of blackness began to cover the sky, but his eyes widened in hushed surprise as he realized that it was not a cloud at all.

Like a swarm of locusts, a seemingly endless army of black-robed Angels dropped out of the three wooden ships in the sky and swept over the city in waves.

Before Morgan could pull himself away from the eerie feeling penetrating his heart, he heard the voice of King Brennan, as though from very far away, until he finally broke out of the trance.

"Gather every last soldier in Rising Mountain and send them out!" King Brennan shouted to Sirio, who flew off of the balcony and into the castle just as quickly as he had come.

Morgan looked back at him, uncertain of what to do or say, after all that had happened. But their attention was pulled away by a great booming sound that came from the city. Morgan's head swung around just in time to see a plume of fire erupt from the East Sanctuary. In a brilliant flash of light, the front of the building had been struck by some Angelic blast, and come tumbling down, spilling ash into the streets as frightened citizens flew away in fear.

But not everyone had made it out in time. The power of the Master's Tear reached out and touched the East Sanctuary, sending a sharp sting into Morgan's chest for each of the lives extinguished inside the building. The army. They were attacking the city!

Before Morgan could think of what to do, he felt a wisp of energy, and a band of at least thirty Angels, sheathed in the red armor of the Royal Guard, shot out of the castle windows all around him and formed a line of bodies, which rushed across the sky toward the black-robed invaders.

All across the city, innocent citizens shut their doors and locked their windows in fear, as two great waves of Angels cut through the air, flying straight toward each other.

At last, the two groups collided in the air and an incredible shockwave of Angelic power rippled over the city, as a blinding light enveloped the entire kingdom. The ground shook violently with the force of hundreds of Angels, the air filled with the terrible roar of battlecries and clashing swords.

~ * ~

Through a screen of smoke, Simon Donnigan emerged from the street below, his golden wings outspread as he rushed up into the air. Beams of cosmic energy shot forth from the hands of a black-robed Angel, who hurled them down at the city below.

Simon spun in the air, in between blasts as he could feel a hail of debris from destroyed buildings rain over him. He grit his teeth when a beam burned through the side of his wing and angrily snatched a cloud of moisture from the air, concentrating it into a liquid spear, which he shot up toward his attacker. Just as the man was about to conjure another blast, he could feel the impossible pressure of a stream of water pierce his chest, knocking him out of the sky, sending him crashing into the stone street below.

But there was no time for Simon to celebrate his victory, as he was barely able to deflect the swing of a sword to his face from another enemy, and his nine friends flying toward him. With a sword in one hand, and a ball of water in another, Simon summoned up all the power at his command, ready to fight till his dying breath, for this city that had forsaken him...

~ * ~

Shards of brick flew from the walls as Aganon slammed the faces of two enemies into the side of the building down below. And, before his third attacker even knew what was happening, his fist came swinging backwards, smacking him across the street with a ferocious scream.

Cherry watched in fear as the tall man fought. She had never seen him like this before. It frightened her more than she would dare admit. But the sight of those foreign Angels, still blocking out the sunlight with their immense numbers, filled her with an even greater fear.

But suddenly, Cherry saw that Aganon had come flying directly at her, with a manic look in his eyes. Cherry dropped to the floor with a cry, but was astonished to see Aganon flying right over her, drilling a kick into another enemy, sending them slamming into another building.

The man was about to strike her from behind and she did not even know. Cherry tried not to let it happen, but as Aganon grabbed her hand and whisked her into the air to escape, tears began to fall from her face. If only she were not so afraid, she thought. She knew she had the power to protect herself, but the fear of losing control and bringing harm to those she cared for was too great to ignore. All she could think now was that she desperately hoped Morgan was safe…

~ * ~

The air above Moralvia grew thick and eerie as Morgan watched the ever-stretching battlefield of the heavens. And through the screen of Royal Guards, fighting relentlessly to protect their kingdom, a number of invading warriors had broken through the line, and made a dash for Rising Mountain.

Into their hands, the warriors summoned spears of cosmic energy, which they hurled out of the air above, toward the castle. A great tidal wave of purple light came slashing through the clouds, threatening to rip the castle apart. But King Brennan stood his ground.

The air around him began to warp unnaturally as his mighty black wings emerged from his back. He thrust his hand up toward his attackers just as the spears were about to strike the castle, and a blast of shadowy energy burst out of his body. When the spears struck the blast, they were sent bouncing off like raindrops hitting an umbrella. Flashes of light echoed in Brennan's eyes as the spears were deflected into the sides of Rising Mountain, where they exploded, sending huge boulders flying out of the mountain and hanging weightlessly in the air. Not one spear had touched the castle.

But Brennan's power waned. Even he, with all his strength, would not be able to hold off so many for so long. He looked up angrily at the invaders as they shot another volley of spears down toward the castle. With all his might, Brennan fired another blast, desperately struggling to keep up with the oncoming attack. Spears bounced away, crashing against the rocks around the castle, but more came, and began to overpower the sweat-soaked king, slowly losing control.

Suddenly, from behind the darkness of Brennan's wings, he felt a tremendous power flash across the balcony. Brennan turned to see that it was Morgan, his hand thrust toward the sky just as his own was, helping to deflect the spears right along with him. The sight of this fifteen-year old boy, holding his own alongside him, wielding such immense power, invigorated his spirit, and he redoubled the intensity of his abilities.

Still, there were too many, and they grew closer and closer to the castle. Soon they would be upon them, and there would be little to do to protect it.

"I must go!"

Brennan turned to face the boy, but by the time his head had spun around, Morgan had already launched off of the balcony, rocketing up into the sky with unmatched speed.

Celestial lightning swirled around his entire body as he flew fearlessly toward the line of warriors attacking the castle. In a matter of seconds, he had thrown a thousand force-filled fists into the faces of all those around him. Brennan looked up in astonishment as they began to surround the blue-winged youth, but every enemy that drew too close was struck down in the wake of a cosmic thunderclap. Smoking bodies fell from the heavens one by one, scattering to ash before they could hit the city below. But more continued to take their place from afar…

~ * ~

A streak of ash flew past Hadar's eyes as he slashed away another foe, struggling to keep up with the enemies that swirled around them on the stone bridge that hung over the West Lake. He, Galvin, and Aganon stood together, surrounding Cherry at the center of the bridge, fighting off all those that came toward them.

With a loud crash, the body of a Moralvian soldier dropped out of the sky just in front of them. Aganon rushed over to the man, whose face was half covered in red, his body trembling in pain. Aganon's pure white wings reached out and wrapped around the two of them as his friends struggled to protect them. A great warmth washed over the man's body from Aganon's hands, slowly beginning to heal his injuries.

"Why?"

Aganon almost did not understand the man, who spoke in a cracked, shaky voice. It was only after he truly looked into his eyes that he realized who it was that was lying before him. It was one of Sirio Nichols' personal soldiers. One of those that must have attacked Simon's house, and helped burn it to the ground. One of those that tried to destroy his friends.

The healing warmth disappeared from his hand…

"You-You are part of Unity… Why would you help me?"

The soldier looked up at the man, whose hand was still hovering over him in uncertainty. Forced back behind Aganon's eyes, there slept a rage that could have easily driven him to curl that hand into a fist. But the thought of Simon flashed through his mind.

"Because," Aganon began, biting back his anger. "Because I am not like you."

A white light flowed from Aganon's hand as he continued repairing the man's wounds.

~ * ~

Simon cried out in pain as a stream of blood trickled down between his eyes. With the swing of his arm, he sent a blade of water sheering through his attacker's body. The man dropped to the ground, vanishing in a cloud of silver at his feet.

But through the dissipating embers, Simon's eyes found a young boy across the street, frightened and alone, with no wings to help protect him, or fly him home. Out of the air above, a robed Angel came flying, brandishing an axe, ready to strike the child. Simon leapt into the air with desperate speed, pushing everything he had left in him to try to get to the child in time, but it was not enough.

Simon reached out in horror as the Angel raised his axe and swung. But an instant before the weapon could touch its target, the attacker was hit by a powerful wave of air, sent crashing to the ground onto his neck.

Sirio's boots crushed the debris on the ground as he landed just between the child and its attacker. Simon stopped himself in the air, as the boy's frantic mother quickly scooped him up, thankful that she had found him, and that someone had saved him.

The light of the fires crackling around him flickered in Simon's eyes as he stared across the street at the man that had hoped to kill him only days earlier. A splash of water surged between his fingers, and he forged them into a powerful whip. Into the palm of Valan's hand swirled a cloud of destructive air. The two stood on opposite ends of the street, each ready to strike the other with deadly attacks.

Suddenly, a rush of energy broke the silence, and the two warriors threw their elemental weapons toward each other simultaneously!

Sirio gasped in shock when he felt the liquid whip shoot past his ear, drilling through the face of a robed Angel behind him. Simon turned his head back just in time to see a current of air explode through an enemy's chest behind him.

The two warriors, both former allies and adversaries, turned back toward each other, realizing that each was fighting the same enemy. And that enemy was not either of them. They looked up at the sea of invading Angels in black robes. Their course was clear.

Without words, Sirio and Simon launched into the air side-by-side, conjuring weapons of wind and water as they headed toward their true enemy…

~ * ~

The light of the sun crept further and further back behind the distant mountains, slowly casting a shadow across the kingdom, though the fires that burned brightly down below still lit the way. As did the flashes of lightning that came screaming out of Morgan's fingers, slicing through his enemies one after another.

King Brennan threw his hands up, fearfully shooting more of his lifeforce into the air, hoping to deflect the incoming spears of energy for at least a few more minutes, while that amazing boy battled the invaders up above. Sweat flowed down Brennan's face, and his breathing wavered, as he at last began to grow weak. Never had his strength been tested in such a way. Very soon, he would be forced to let go.

"No!" Morgan shouted. Brennan was losing his ability to protect the castle, and there were still so many coming toward him with weapons, wielding terrible powers, each trying to destroy him with more determination than the last.

"Do not resist."

The voice reached out to him in his mind, as bolts of lightning flew through him and into the bodies of those that approached him. The power of the Master's Tear had guided the voice to him, and it only intensified his fear. The voice was so familiar, but as he struggled to keep up against the warriors that swung swords at him, he resisted the urge to reach out to whoever had sent it.

"The battle is lost. The Alorium are victorious."

"Silence!"

A burst of lightning lashed out and exploded an enemy's face right in front of Morgan. But just before the man's head flew apart, Morgan realized that it had belonged to someone much younger than he would have expected. And when Morgan reached out with the Master's Tear, he found that the essence of nearly all those flying in the air around him belonged to Angels that were too young to bare wings. And yet they flew, and their wings were as real as his own. They were like him!

But why then? Morgan thought. *Why would you, who are said to be the ones who lead Angelkind into the future, commit such terrible crimes against us?*

An awful chill skittered down Morgan's spine as a voice answered what he believed were his own private thoughts.

"Because it is our birthright!"

Morgan's eyes widened in fear as he could sense a power of unspeakable strength tear through the sky. The air he breathed was snatched right out of his lungs as he threw himself out of the way, and a massive wall of energy ripped through the very fabric of the air, headed straight for Rising Mountain.

The beating of Morgan's heart was silenced under the oppressive weight of the blast that hit the floating land, and in the wake of cosmic, blue fire, split the entire mountain in two.

King Brennan would have cried out if the air around him hadn't been obliterated by the blast, which tossed him through wall after wall of the castle like a child's plaything, until he slammed into the stone floor of his own throne room.

Streams of spectral smoke rose from the king's blood-soaked body as he gasped for the first remnants of air that at last returned to his lungs. With frantic, unfocused vision, he looked up in physical and mental shock at the sight of one half of his castle slowly floating away from him, and a great, gaping wound in the walls and ceiling, where he had been thrown, and the flaming stone had been blasted.

Morgan emerged through a cloud with trembling wings, barely able to comprehend what he had just witnessed. A blurred figure darted past him from the leading airship, straight for the castle. And as the lone figure passed, a sudden feeling of sickness flushed through him. Blood raced through his veins unnaturally. His stomach churned. It was as though hatred and anger had been twisted into a physical aura, which permeated the air around that figure as it flew.

"Alorium Hai!" the robed warriors suddenly shouted.

Morgan knew those words. Through the knowledge bestowed upon him by the power of the Master's Tear, he understood immediately that it was an ancient utterance, spoken in the original tongue of the Angels, during the time of the first Book of the Angelic Text. The phrase was an affirmation of faith, and devotion, to the Alorium. But Morgan knew very few people that even believed in the Alorium, much less felt strongly enough to invoke such an ancient phrase.

There was only one thing left to do. Though fear had reduced his incredible flying speed to a fraction of what it once was, Morgan did not turn back, as he followed the figure into the approaching night, toward the castle.

Morgan could feel the Angel's power more strongly, and as he drew nearer, the weight of his hatred grew more intense. Through floating debris, he soared, until at last, he found King Brennan, struggling to even pull himself up onto one knee, having been nearly destroyed by the power of that massive blast.

As Morgan approached, startled by the pain of seeing his former father in such a pathetic state, he slowly realized that they were all the same. The one who spoke to him in his thoughts. The one who did this to the king. And the one who brought this army to their kingdom. The Master's Tear shook violently beneath his shirt, reacting like never before to that voice, which Morgan desperately tried to shut out of his mind. It was overpowering. He feared that, if he gave in to the voice for even an instant, his very essence could be consumed by it.

"At last we meet."

Morgan's head snapped back. As he stood between King Brennan and the hooded man emerging from the shadows, his fear knew no equal for what he was about to see.

His wings. The hooded man's wings, which stretched up around him like a banner, were the color of sapphire. Morgan knew it before the Angel pulled away his hood, but the sight of his face turned his skin pale. The Angel removed the hood from over his head to reveal that he looked identical to Morgan.

"Hello, Morgan," he said with a smile. "I'm Kiran Ellison. I'm your brother..."

STEP 14
FALLEN ANGEL

Morgan struggled to catch his breath as visions of the past came flooding into his mind, and he slowly began to grasp all that was being revealed to him in mere moments. He had a twin. A brother. A child that was smuggled out of the castle by one of the king's servants and taken to a faraway land to be raised by her and her new husband. They were the Ellisons. They were Kiran's adoptive parents.

Never in life did the Ellisons believe that Kiran and Morgan would ever cross paths. But the two of them always knew. Somehow, deep inside of them, they knew that this day would come. And the power rattling in Morgan's amulet intensified that feeling even more.

"It's true," Kiran said, as he pulled something from behind his shirt. Morgan knew what it was before he saw it.

The third and final Master's Tear hung around Kiran's neck, filling him with the same knowledge and powers of sight that

Morgan possessed. But unlike Morgan, Kiran had worn the jewel for many years, and gave off an aura of authority whenever he used it. Morgan was still struggling to keep from being overwhelmed by its seemingly limitless power.

"You knew this day would come," Kiran continued. "That the two of us would stand face to face again, after nearly 15 years of separation. Every step we took in our lives, we were marching toward this end. And the final step is upon us now."

Morgan struggled not to show fear at the presence of the young man that wore his face, but he could not shut him out of his mind. Kiran suffocated the room with a cold, dark energy. Morgan could sense without turning around that King Brennan, clinging to consciousness from the pain of his injuries, was stunned at the sight of the boy that looked so much like his only son.

"Tell me, brother," Morgan said with a cracked voice. "To what end are we supposed to be marching toward?"

"The three Master's Tears are together at last. I know you're still having trouble processing their knowledge, but you must know by now that the Tears are meant to open the path to Earth."

Upon the very mention of Earth, a frenzy of images was transmitted to Morgan's thoughts from his amulet. Images of a place beyond the reach of normal Angels, where men and women without wings led their lives, in towers of iron and glass, and traveled in chariots of steel. A place he knew the Angelic Text taught that Angelkind were meant to watch over and protect.

"You want to go to Earth?" Morgan asked in surprise. With all the negative energy he felt from his doppelganger, the last thing he expected was to hear that he wanted to return the Angels to Earth to bring help and protection to its people.

"Of course," Kiran replied. "It is there where we will make our new home. After we've eliminated the vermin."

Morgan took a step back. He did not need to ask what he meant. He could see his true intentions in his thoughts, and it filled him with a dread like nothing else ever had.

"You intend to destroy them… All of Earthkind, everywhere."

"We are Angels… We are Alorium… We alone decide the future of the universe. We are the Master Race. And, as leaders of that new race, you and I will sweep away all those who oppose our authority."

Morgan looked at his brother with horror in his eyes. Kiran quickly sensed that the young man that stood before him was not happy to see him, or hear his words. Morgan could feel Kiran's mind penetrating his own. He struggled to keep him out of his thoughts, but the more he resisted, the more difficult it became. It seemed effortless for Kiran. In moments, Morgan saw it.

It was the day Kiran found his adoptive parents lying dead in the street, slowly drifting into the air in a cloud of silver ash, after having been stoned to death by the citizens of Jeruma City.

"They killed them," Kiran said. "Because of the color of their wings."

"Kiran," Morgan forced out, still fighting to keep up whatever wall he could maintain in his thoughts. "What they did to the Ellisons was wrong. But that doesn't mean that—"

"And do you know what I did then?... I impaled those pigs on the tips of my own wings!"

Morgan shouted out in horror as he could feel exactly what Kiran had felt when he stabbed his wings into the bodies of the two officers in the street. He experienced the horrible sensation as their bodies turned to ash and sprinkled down between Kiran's feathers, as though they were Morgan's own. He could feel their lives extinguish like blowing out a candle. And they were not Kiran's only victims that day.

With untold power, Kiran's hatred had exploded all across Jeruma City, the place he had once called home, and claimed the lives of nearly half the land's inhabitants. All those that were fortunate (or unfortunate) enough to rise from the rubble immediately dropped to their knees at the sight of him—this boy of only seven years, with tall, blue wings. This "gift from the Master." This Alorium...

"Stop," Morgan mumbled, his body shaking, sweat rushing down his face. But Kiran did not stop. He carried on, showing Morgan one awful image after another, along his venomous road toward making himself leader of an army of warriors, supported by a vast alliance of disciples. And all the lives he cut short in the terrifying process.

"Stop," Morgan said again... Kiran did not listen.

"STOP!"

A massive build-up of anger erupted from Morgan's body, and

an unprepared Kiran suddenly found himself being launched backwards by his brother's power. Morgan struggled to breathe as Kiran's consciousness was forcibly removed from his own.

Kiran's body twirled as it was thrown across the room, but quickly halted itself upside-down in the air. The young man smiled with delight. It was the first time he had felt it. That same anger that had fueled Kiran's powers for so long. The anger that Morgan had only just begun to tap into. What would eventually make him just as powerful, and just as feared as he was.

"You're strong," Kiran laughed. "But there's much I can teach you. And I'll do it gladly."

"No," Morgan shouted. "You have nothing to teach me. Because you're insane. You have nothing to offer me. Or anyone else."

"I doubt very much Cherry would agree with that statement."

Morgan's eyes narrowed at the girl's mention.

"You may be able to hide your feelings for her from the others, but not from me. There are so many things that I could give her. You truly have no idea."

"You… Stay away from her!"

The room began to shake in response to the rise in power as Morgan lifted off of the floor and darted across the room toward Kiran with Angelic lightning gathering into his fist…

~ * ~

Streams of water whipped furiously around Simon, as he sent them ripping through the bodies of his enemies. Like leaves from a tree in the wind, his adversaries fell around him in pieces, quickly dematerializing as they hit the ground below him. But they were simply replaced by more of Kiran's warriors.

In the wake of a swift wind, three warriors were blasted to the ground behind Simon, as Sirio struggled to keep going, but with varied success. A spear had been driven through his left shoulder, paralyzing that arm, and with his one free hand, he struggled to keep fighting alongside his one ally in sight.

A cloak of shadow covered the starless night sky.

Before Simon realized what was happening, he was struck down by some nameless blast and sent colliding with Sirio. The two fell out of the air and slammed into the stone street below. Simon quickly jumped back up, but was halted by the razor edge of a sword at his throat. A second later, there were five more of them pointed at him and Sirio.

Simon looked all around him to find that the fighting had died down. Warriors descended from the skies, holding the last surviving Moralvians at the edge of a blade.

It was not long before many others were forced out of their homes and thrown to the street in a great group around Simon and Sirio. He turned to see that Cherry and Aganon were forced to the ground on the outside of the group, surrounded on all sides by Kiran's followers. Galvin and Hadar were not too far away from them on the opposite side, gripping terrible wounds, and covered in dirt.

There was little any of them could do now without endangering more innocents, especially in such a weakened state. Simon let out a painful sigh. They were defeated.

Sirio looked up to find that one of the robed invaders had stepped forward and removed the hood from over his face. Whispers of surprise echoed in the background as Sirio's eyes narrowed, realizing that the young man was much younger than they expected. Too young, they thought, to have wings.

The man raised his hand and into his grasp he forged a pulsating blade of spectral light, the mere touch of which could sheer a tree in two.

"My name is General Kyler," the man started, "You are alive now because our divine leader, Kiran Ellison, wishes to give you one last chance. To pledge your devotion to his cause, and follow the true path, which he has laid out for us all. Those who do not comply—who choose to embrace evil—will be executed in his name!"

~ * ~

Morgan rushed through the air toward Kiran, filling his fist with power, fueled purely by his anger for what Kiran had done. But Kiran did not flinch. He simply watched with a smile as the boy cut through the air in a blue blur, hurling his fist at him at immeasurable speed.

Morgan cried out in astonished pain when his fist connected with Kiran's arm, causing a shockwave of energy to rock through the entire castle. It felt as though he had driven his fist into a wall of solid rock. Kiran's smile grew larger as he whipped his free hand around and smashed it across Morgan's face.

King Brennan watched in shock as Morgan's body was blasted back across the room just as quickly as it had come, and slammed through the wall just next to where he was sitting. But what struck Brennan even more was that he could sense no decline in Morgan's essence. In fact, he felt it more strongly than he ever had before!

Brennan turned just in time to see Morgan walk through the hole he had just blown into the wall. The dust on his body seemed to float away on its own.

It was clear to Brennan now that this boy, whatever he was, had become something more than an ordinary Angel. He did not believe in the books that told of the Alorium. But he knew that a being such as this had to have been born of something more than what *he* was. And it made his blood run cold.

Morgan slowly walked past the king with fury in his eyes, fixed solely on Kiran.

"Very good," Kiran said, wrapping his wings around himself like a cloak. "You're learning how your anger brings you strength. You're on your way to finding out who you really are. My equal. My ally."

Morgan stopped. Kiran could suddenly feel his power decrease.

A pause.

"No," Morgan said at last. "I will never be like you. Consumed with hatred and anger at everyone and everything. What happened to you as a child, in the place you were raised, made you a monster. You forgot what an Angel is supposed to be like. But me… What happened to me as a child, in this place where I was raised, has made me into something else entirely… You won't make me into what you are… I'm better than that."

Brennan closed his eyes in silent surprise at Morgan's words. Never had he heard his son speak this way. About his upbringing. About how his world was shaped. A single tear fell from the king's eye, as he realized he had made a terrible mistake…

But Kiran did not feel the same reverence for his brother. A terrible feeling of sickness fell over Brennan as he sensed Kiran's anger increase. The throne room began to tremble in response to the power flooding out of him in waves.

Their battle had only just begun…

~ * ~

Through tremoring eyes, Cherry watched as more men and women were gathered and tossed into the group at the center of the street. The young faces of those who corralled them only made it worse. What terrible thing could have caused them all to be led to such malice? How could one voice hold that much sway over their hearts?

"Do you denounce your old life, and pledge to follow the true path?"

Aganon turned to find that the man General Kyler spoke to was a Royal Guardian. The very same Guardian that he had healed on the battlefield only hours earlier. Since then, the man had received a great many more injuries, and was in no condition to give battle to anyone anymore.

The soldier raised his eyes to the man with the glowing weapon in his hand, crackling with Angelic power, and said "No."

A flash of light struck the soldier's throat, and in an instant, he dropped to the ground and scattered into ashes at Kyler's feet. A roar of fearful cries rang out from the crowd as the invader thoughtlessly executed the man. Aganon tightened a fist at his side, a tidal wave of rage held back behind his eyes.

"Now," Kyler said, as he approached the young woman next in line. "Do you denounce your old life, and pledge to follow the true path?"

Clinging to the woman's trembling body were two young boys. She held tightly to her children, overcome with fear.

"I will not ask again," Kyler persisted.

With a broken voice, the woman nodded her head, and said "Yes…"

Kyler smiled and moved on.

But the next face he saw did not look up at him with the same fear and despair. It was the face of Hadar Ackson. And he stared into the eyes of the general with icy contempt.

"Do you denounce your old life, and pledge to follow the true path?"

Next to Hadar sat his brother, Galvin, who turned to his brother in fear, as he realized he was not answering. He knew Hadar too well to expect his pride not to interfere with his judgment. Even against death itself, he expected Hadar to resist.

Galvin could do nothing but watch as his stubborn brother would most certainly say or do something to destroy himself.

"…. Yes."

Galvin stared at Hadar with a gaping jaw, in utter astonishment. In all the battles—all the conflicts—he and his brother had fought through, Hadar's impudent, stubborn ways could not be suppressed. His pride ruled his actions, and he fought passionately against any odds, even knowing that he may die for the ideals he stood for.

But now, as Galvin watched tears stream down Hadar's face, he could not believe what he had just witnessed. His brother held himself back. Hadar's life was preserved. But his ideals were shattered.

Even as Kyler moved on, stepping directly in front of him, Galvin stared at his younger brother. The very idea of his yielding was unbelievable.

"Hadar," Galvin said.

Hadar did not respond. Nor did he look at him. He sat there, weary-eyed and lost. Galvin could not bare to see him reduced to this. Though Hadar had done what he had hoped him to do, it was not what he *expected* him to do.

"Now," Kyler spoke. "Do you denounce your old life, and pledge to follow the true path?"

Galvin turned his head with a defiant glare. "The answer is no."

At last, Hadar looked to his brother, in a mixture of terror of confusion.

Before Kyler could raise his blade of light to attack, Galvin had already leapt forth and tackled him to the ground with an angry growl.

In moments, Aganon, Simon, Sirio, and many others jumped into the air, battlecries of rebellion bellowing all through the streets in a sudden frenzy.

Through pain and uncertainty, the Moralvians fought valiantly against their oppressors with an unrelenting strength, the likes of which their enemies could not have expected.

Galvin cried out as he was thrown into the air from Kyler's boot. The general quickly spun himself into the air, his shimmering blade cutting through the wind toward his insolent target.

Hadar watched in amazement as his brother's wings stretched out behind him, waves of restless power flowing out of his body. Hadar saw no other option. He flew up next to his brother and conjured a sword into his hand, ready to fight at his side, against any danger.

But as Kyler and the Acksons rushed through the air toward each other, Cherry stood up in fear at the sight of the young woman with her two young children. Frozen with dread, they sat huddled on the ground between the three warriors hurtling across the battlefield, about to collide, and perhaps destroy them all.

The memory of Cherry's mother flashed into her mind.

Suddenly, moments before Kyler could strike his foes, the sword of light in his hand seemed to vanish from his grasp. He stopped in the air, looking down at his empty hand in surprise.

And before he realized what was happening, he felt the sting of Hadar's blade hissing through his body. With a terrible cry, Kyler went twirling out of the sky, exploding into a cloud of ash as he slammed into the ground below.

A glowing blade appeared in Cherry's hand as the embers of silver ash fluttered past the mother and her children. And, as her crimson wings flowed from her back, a tremendous power was unleashed. A power over which she held complete control.

A great fleet of robed warriors came rushing out of the distance toward the Moralvians, each wielding an equally deadly weapon of cosmic power. Simon blocked a sword with his own, quickly realizing they were about to be overrun once again.

But before he could act, a sudden rush of energy shot through the streets. Through a veil of ashes, Simon could feel that it all came from his young red-haired friend.

Just as the invaders began to approach, they found that their Angelic gifts had been stolen. And instead of attacking the defiant Moralvians, they were rendered powerless against them. Their essence had been utterly suffocated by Cherry's own. Their power was now hers to wield.

The warriors watched as Cherry planted her glowing saber into the ground and the earth trembled. The street below them erupted, swallowing them up in an explosion of debris. Dirt and rock scattered through the air, as the invaders were thrown about, crashing lifelessly here and there.

Sirio sent a blade of air slashing through an enemy with his one strong arm, but was startled by a powerful sense of intuition that commanded his attention toward the distant sky.

Suddenly, the entire battlefield was rocked by an immense thunderclap that rippled out of the castle of Rising Mountain, shattering windows throughout the kingdom below.

Sirio's eyes widened. Rising Mountain hung in the air in shambles, ripped in half by some unimaginable force, the likes of which he never thought possible. Somewhere in that place, surrounded by enemies, was his king. And he, overwhelmed by adversaries, was unable to protect him. As Sirio gathered an angry wind around him, he realized his father's legacy was about to end with him…

~ * ~

Brennan's eyes widened in astonishment as he struggled to follow what was happening before him. Kiran and Morgan moved with such horrifying speed that the king's eyes could barely catch their movements, as the two swung hundreds of fists back and forth through the throne room over the span of only seconds.

Morgan could feel the fabric of the air ripple around him as his arms blasted through them toward his enemy. Kiran watched with a smirk of amusement as he continued to deflect each attack with utter ease. Even now, as every thrust of Morgan's fist sent a splinter of power drilling holes into the walls, he remained unburdened by his twin's growing strength.

"What happened?" Kiran asked, as a chasm was split into the floor beneath them. "What happened to all of that power you had? Where did it go?"

"Be silent!" Morgan shouted, tossing up another failed kick. Morgan could feel his strength continuing to grow, the Master's Tear slowly magnifying his Angelic power. But it was useless against that unimaginable rage bubbling beneath the surface of Kiran's heart, breaking out of his body with such appalling grace.

"I see," Kiran said, deflecting another kick. "I will have to EDUCATE YOU!"

Morgan gasped for air as he threw forth a punch, but suddenly felt Kiran's fist smash its way right past his own and land at his chest.

Brennan dropped into a slumber at the mere vibration brought on by such an attack, which sent Morgan launching backward as though by a catapult, shooting through the gash in the castle, right out of Rising Mountain in half a second.

Morgan struggled to breathe as his body was ripped through the air with such undeniable force that he was unable to stop himself. As he was torn backwards through sheets of cold, the clouds around him were scattered by the mere frantic flapping of his wings.

Morgan was a blue dart that rocketed through the sky over the city, whose cries echoed across the entire land as he spun wildly out of control.

And somewhere down below, Simon Donnigan looked up past the enemies that fought around him, and knew it. Though he could not see it with his eyes, he could feel it. That blue blur that set the sky ablaze with its movements, flashing across nearly the entire city. It was his one true Alorium.

But before Simon could muster another thought, he could see Morgan's body slam into the lower front of one of the great airships that hung in the air. The impact sent a shiver of power skittering across the kingdom, as faces from both sides of the battle below turned to the sky above.

Morgan's cries were drowned out by the wall of sound that erupted all around him, as his body was blasted through walls and wood and metal. He could feel the essence of those that remained inside the ship, who scattered into the air, struggling to escape the fragments of debris that nearly destroyed them.

Out of every possible exit, the invaders came flying out of the ship as it was forced into a massive lateral spin that shook the clouds.

Morgan knew not how long it had been, but his injuries had knocked him into a brief slumber. He opened his eyes to find himself somewhere in the middle of the half-destroyed ship as it moved uncontrollably in the air. He turned, looking out through the broken window at his side, watching the blur of buildings whip past his view. One of which was the Tower of Light.

But the next thing he saw through the window was the quick image of the two other airships that hung in the air. The back of the vessel was about to swing itself into them.

A surge of power flushed through Morgan as he jumped to his feet and threw a hand toward the window, causing a great burst of air to carve a hole into it, which he quickly rushed through. Fighting past the pain of the injuries that covered his body, he released his wings into the air and darted out of the airship with all the speed he could muster.

Morgan's feet landed at the top of the Tower of Light as he helplessly watched the leading airship collide with another, which was forced into the third. Wood and steel was tossed in all directions as the three ships were evacuated by the last of their passengers.

But suddenly, as the airships began to lose control and tip down toward the city below, Morgan could feel a swell of lifeforce that quickly approached from behind. He turned, expecting to see someone appearing from afar, but instead, found that he was already upon him. Kiran let out a laugh as he sent a foot drilling into the side of his brother's face from above, sending him shooting down from the tower only moments after he had landed there.

Kiran's boots touched the roof of the tower, crossing his arms as the three airships came crashing down through buildings behind him, spilling out across the streets. Clouds of debris rolled across the city in a seemingly never-ending parade of destruction. Kiran watched as Morgan's body collided with the ground below.

Morgan looked up through blurred vision at the distant image of his double staring down at him from above with a smile. With all the terrible pains that racked his body, he could sense that Kiran was pleased. That he knew, with all the power still flowing through Morgan, he would not die from his injuries. It would only succeed in making him angrier, and unlock his true power.

Through the power of his amulet, Morgan peered all around him to feel the despair in the hearts of all those that had witnessed it. The destruction of their homes by the collapse of the airships. The invasion of their kingdom by Kiran's army of oppressors. With all that was against them, there seemed to be no way to escape.

"Now," Kiran said, though not through his lips. "Now you understand that you cannot defeat me. The only chance for yourself, and for these common-blooded fools is to join us. Baptize yourself in the darkness of your own heart, and use it to reshape this world into one worthy of the Master. As children of the Master Race, that is our destiny."

Kiran looked out at the broken kingdom and his overwhelming essence pierced the thoughts of all that stood within its borders. They all heard his words, and could sense the unstoppable resolve in his blackened heart.

Simon looked out into the distance as a tear dropped from his eye. Aganon, Sirio, Cherry, Galvin and Hadar all gathered around him in anguish. They could feel Kiran's essence as clearly as though it were their own. And a smile stretched over his face.

"No."

Kiran's smile fell away.

"What?" Kiran said aloud.

"I said no."

Kiran peered down toward the former prince still sprawled on the street below with an angry gaze.

"I will not join you," Morgan said. "You said it was our duty to reshape the world. But I will have no part in that if it means reshaping my own heart. I will die here before I become what you are. I will die…"

Cracks suddenly began to form at the peak of the tower at Kiran's feet. He curled a hand into a fist. The blue of his eyes turned to an empty, bottomless black.

"Very well," Kiran said, his vengeful voice echoing in the air. "The path to the future will be painted with your blood…"

Morgan laid there, his face sullied, his clothing ripped, staring up into the sky, dumfounded. His muscles ached in ways he never knew they could. He was certain that several bones within him had broken. He was not certain if he could even stand on both legs. With all his powers, fueled by his hatred for this man that looked just like him, he still was not strong enough. He could never learn to be as Kiran was, to hate as much as he did. He feared he could never survive a battle with this man who wrapped himself in anger as though it were a cloak.

But Morgan had little time to think, as he could feel his brother dropping out of the sky with a furious battlecry. Kiran's hatred ignited in disgust as he channeled his malevolence into his foot, ready to drive it right through his brother's body.

~ * ~

"He cannot win."

Simon's head snapped around to find that it was Cherry that

had spoken, as she stepped forward, staring out toward the Tower of Light.

"What?" Aganon asked, struggling to hold fast to his beliefs in the face of such amazement.

"Morgan," she said, in that soft voice they all remembered. "He cannot win like that…"

"Cherry," Simon started. "What do you mean?"

"You must feel it by now. Kiran wants nothing more right now than to kill Morgan in the worst possible way. And he will feel little remorse for it when he's finished. That is what he is. But Morgan. That is not who Morgan is… He cannot win like that. He cannot defeat Kiran with his hatred."

Sirio stood in confusion, desperate for a voice of reassurance, as he could feel that awesome power descending from the tower.

~ * ~

Morgan watched silently as Kiran came rushing down toward him. He struggled to move, but a great pain pierced his legs, and one of his arms refused to lift on its own. Morgan looked up in fear as his twin came upon him.

But suddenly, the image of Cherry flashed into his thoughts, and his body went spinning out of the way at the last instant. A plume of smoke and debris erupted beneath Kiran's boot, but Morgan landed on his back just outside of it, along the wall of the Sanctuary outside the Tower of Light.

Tears began to appear in Morgan's eyes. It was Cherry. She had saved him.

"Finally," Cherry said. In his heart, he could hear her. "I am able to return the favor."

Kiran's growl of anger sent tremors rippling through the streets, as he began slowly marching toward his brother.

"Now," Cherry continued. "…Get up."

As though of its own free will, Morgan's body pulled itself up from the ground. Morgan lifted a hand and looked at it in wonder as he could feel a new power coursing through his veins. The power was not of his own making. Through that power, he could feel the essence of that young woman, as well as all those around her. He looked around him, overwhelmed by the warmth that flooded over him, from the lifeforce of nearly every Angel in the entire kingdom.

It was Cherry's gift. A power that could not have come from hatred or anger. Through Cherry, all of Moralvia saw all that she had seen, and what she had felt for this man, and delivered unto him all the strength they could muster. And in return, he could feel all that they had seen and felt. Including his father, peering down from a half-broken balcony at Rising Mountain, struggling to hold himself up as the fate of his kingdom was decided.

As Morgan turned back toward Kiran, he looked upon him with new eyes. He could see more than ever before. More than any Master's Tear could ever show him. The entire evolution of every particle in his body. The very core to his soul. The rhythm of the essence flowing inside him. The seed of his hatred. Everything, in such majestic clarity.

As Kiran marched closer, a shimmer of pure, white light danced above Morgan and swirled into a glowing ring over his head.

Kiran poured his hatred into his fist and thrust it at his brother with all that he had. Morgan simply blinked and Kiran hit nothing but a wall of Angelic energy, shattering his hand. Kiran threw a cosmic blast from his free hand. Morgan's gaze caused it to fire back on itself.

Morgan watched as Kiran was launched into the air by his own attack, the blast devastating him in ways no one had ever done in his life. The former prince lifted from the ground to follow Kiran's body, which flipped endlessly up into the sky, slashing through clouds, higher and higher.

Dripping wet from the moisture of the clouds, racked with injury, Kiran struggled to hold himself in the air. But he had lost the strength to completely halt himself. His spirit was consumed by his brother's presence. He could feel his essence all around him, smothering his own dark emanations. He did not understand. How could Morgan have become so powerful without fighting the way he did? There was no power greater than what Kiran had conjured. Or so he thought.

Morgan appeared before Kiran in a flash, too quickly for his brother's eyes to notice until he was already right in front of his face. Kiran tried to fight, but every attack he threw at Morgan only weakened him. Exerting no effort at all, Morgan deflected his movements with tiny flickers of power, as he hung in the air, watching his twin, almost amused by his attempts to harm him.

"Wait," Morgan suddenly said, as though he knew what Kiran was about to do.

But Kiran refused to listen. Morgan could see, in limitless detail, the horrors of Kiran's life, which he gathered up in one great mass of negative power. It was more than he had ever conjured up at once. So much that there would be nothing left to give once he released it from his hands. And he did not care. As long as he destroyed this man that wore his face, who threatened his authority.

"Now...you die..."

Kiran thrust his hands forward, and a blaze of unrestrained rage burned across the heavens with cataclysmic force.

Morgan raised his hand, and silence struck the World. For a brief instant, that single moment in time was suspended, and all Angels everywhere could feel the ever-reaching essence of this blue-winged man, whose power stretched beyond the limits of their imagination.

Kiran's blast was reflected back on itself. His cries were silenced by the terrible force that sheared through his body. A force that scattered him to nothingness in the air, leaving nothing left but the jewel that had hung from his neck.

Morgan silently dropped his head in sorrow as the light of the morning sun had begun pouring in from behind the distant mountains, touching the two halves of Rising Mountain, and the valley below. He raised his arm and into his hand flew the amulet.

The Tower of Light shimmered brightly in the center of the city. As Morgan lowered back into the streets, he found that a great army of Angels, both from Moralvia and from elsewhere, had dropped to one knee. Their prince had come home…

STEP 15
DUST

The glow of the blue jewels shimmered majestically in the eyes of Sirio Nichols, who stood in awe of their splendor as they sat together at the ivory altar. He fell into a bow and brought his hands together in prayer.

Kneeling there in the empty chamber, he began to weep for his father. If any other man had told him of the tragedy that had befell Kaster Nichols, he would not have believed it.

But when the former prince Morgan fought above the city, Sirio's essence was intermingled with his, just as it was for everyone. And in his heart, he witnessed Morgan's memories as though they were his own. Kaster Nichols had been destroyed by the very man Sirio had fought to protect for nearly all his adult life.

What treachery, he thought, struggling to contain his rage. What terrible hypocrisy the king had carried on all those years. And he had blindly supported his every step. What then, he wondered, did that say of himself?

Drying his eyes on a sleeve, he whispered a prayer for forgiveness, and turned to walk out. There was little time left. Soon, the ceremony would begin. And he intended to make his presence known…

~ * ~

"How is it you, of all people, do not know how to tie a sash?"

Simon pushed up his glasses at his friend's statement and frowned. It was a great irony that Aganon, whom he had never seen dress formally in all his life, knew exactly how to tie a sash across his ceremonial garb, and Simon did not.

"Be kind and help an old friend," Simon replied.

"Hopeless," Aganon laughed, snatching the white sash from Simon's desk.

As Aganon tied the ribbon over his suit, Simon looked out the newly-remade window of his house. A warm sunlight poured in from above. The two of them had fixed the window themselves no less than three days earlier. At long last, the place had begun to feel like a home again.

"It is strange," Aganon said. "You still believe wholeheartedly that the Alorium were to bring a new peace back to the World. That the gathering of the three jewels would return the Master to us."

"Yes."

"None of this has happened. In fact, very little has happened since that day. When the three jewels were brought together.

Although Kiran Ellison's followers were disbanded—at least those that we know of—not much else has occurred. And yet still you believe."

"…Yes."

"Fascinating."

"Indeed… Now come. We cannot miss the ceremony."

~ * ~

"Can't catch me!" Gwen shouted gleefully as she ran through the grassy fields outside Moralvia, and her three friends hopelessly tried to keep up.

Gwen was always the quickest of the four children. Gwen laughed as her hair flew freely about her in the wind.

So much had changed, but this was one thing that would stay the same. In any race, the others knew they would not be able to beat her. But of course, it still did not stop them from trying.

From beyond a distant hill, a voice could be heard over the laughter of the four children. Gwen turned to find that her uncles had appeared atop the hill, waving.

"Gwen," Hadar yelled from afar. "It is time to go. Say goodbye to your friends!"

"Yes uncle," Gwen answered.

She quickly bid her companions farewell and ran off toward the Ackson Brothers. The three watched wide-eyed as the young girl lifted into the air and a pair of wondrous brown wings stretched out from her back and took her to the sky.

Gwen, Hadar, and Galvin flew side-by-side as they returned to the city, hoping not to arrive late to the ceremony. It was the first time since that great battle that the king would speak to his people. And there was nothing that would keep the Ackson Brothers from witnessing that.

~ * ~

Galvin peered over the edge of the building rooftop and was astonished to see the number of Angels gathered in the city square. Nearly twice as many as the last ceremony of this sort. A radiant sun glowed majestically upon a sea of men and women dressed in white silk. From all across Moralvia and beyond, they had come for the service in honor of one person's memory.

Next to Galvin sat Hadar, his legs swinging irreverently off the edge of the roof. And on his opposite side sat young Gwen, her legs swinging right along with his own. He looked up to see Galvin's reaction to what he thought was an adorable moment, only to be met with a disapproving eye. Hadar and Gwen quickly straightened their posture and watched.

To temper the crowd, a brigade of police officers in ceremonial dress stood before the great empty platform surrounded on all sides by onlookers. Among those men was Officer Simon Donnigan, who stood proudly with the ivory seal of the law fastened tightly against the sash that stretched over his suit.

The crowd stirred as fingers pointed up to the sky in

anticipation for the arrival of the Royal Guardians. And out of a golden patch of clouds, they appeared. Four Royal Guardians, with Sirio Nichols leading the caravan, each one holding a section of the silver chariot between them.

The Guardians landed atop the platform, gently setting down the chariot.

With a trembling hand, Sirio pulled forth the shimmering horn of the Craft Family. He looked down at the instrument and could not remember the number of times he had used it to summon the attention of the king's subjects. And as he brought it to his lips, he knew that it would be the last time he would ever give his breath to the same cause.

With that, Sirio began to blow, sending a powerful sound pouring through the streets. The very hint of its commanding voice shot a wave of citizens to their knees in respect.

Three men stepped forth from the chariot, each with the Angelic Text in hand. They were Clerics of the Sanctuary. Immediately, they summoned their wings and the pages of the books flipped open to the funeral passage. In unison, they began to recite the sacred words in their ancient tongue. As their words drifted out among the crowd, wings began to flow from the backs of the citizens, in respect for the lost. Wings of all colors.

At the front of the crowd knelt Mr. English, his grey wings outstretched, quietly awaiting His Majesty's appearance, though not as humbly as once before. He knew that whatever he was about to hear, it would not please him. In fact, it quite possibly would mean the ruination of his way of life.

At last, the king revealed himself. Through a white silk curtain, King Morgan emerged from the chariot and looked out at the boundless number that knelt before him. Stepping out just behind him was the ruby-eyed Cherry, a ring of white flowers in her hair.

Sirio watched quietly at Morgan's side, surprised to find that the king wore a sad look across his face. Though it was not for the public's ears, it was well-known among Morgan's inner circle that his father had sought to execute him. So why then would Morgan weep for the loss of a man he had already renounced long ago? Perhaps, he thought, it was simply an act, to conceal his true feelings for the late king.

The Clerics completed their recital and closed their books.

With a gesture, Morgan raised the crowd from the ground, and called the attention of every eye that surrounded him. A spell of nervousness trickled over him as he realized it was time to speak. All around him, faces waited silently for the first word of their king. The future of their society would begin with his next breath.

Morgan felt Cherry's fingers slip between his own and their essence intermingled.

He looked out at the crowd, and smiled…

Printed in the United States
217363BV00001B/166/P